After

The

Rain

A.B. Turner

ISBN: **9798864849170**

DEDICATION

"...hope inspires us to dream, to reach for the stars, and to believe that anything is possible. It is the light that guides us through the darkest of times." – *Athena May Bower.*

.

CONTENTS

ACKNOWLEDGMENTS

As always, I gratefully acknowledge my wonderful editor, my small but mighty family. But also, the wonderful circle of authors and book lovers who offer their help and advice in such a caring and constructive way.

CHAPTER ONE

The rain fell in torrents, drenching the world around me
with relentless intensity. Like an iced tear from the
heavens, each droplet collided with my skin, leaving a
glistening trail in its wake. The darkness felt amplified by
the wild shadows dancing in the ethereal glow of
streetlights and their shimmering reflections on the wet
pavement. I walked alone; footsteps muffled by the
raindrops as they hammered into the stone.

At last, I had found the courage to leave the house that,
over time, had become more like a prison. All I had
brought with me was the desperate knowledge that it
wouldn't be long before I would be free from the
suffocating grip of my thoughts. Each step felt heavy,
burdened by the weight of the intense depression; the bleak
oceanic pressure threatened to shatter me with every step.
Somehow, it seemed the rain understood the dull ache
within me as it cascaded down, washing away the flimsy
mask of sanity I had worn for far too long. Once vibrant
and alive, the city now appeared desolate and empty,
mirroring the void that consumed me. I heard a lone bell of
St. Anthony's, its ominous low tone in sharp contrast to the

joyous peal that accompanied Mass every Sunday. After eleven slow, almost funereal chimes, it fell silent, leaving me to walk alone with my heart echoing the rhythm of the falling rain.

My sodden clothes clung to my body as I trudged through the flooded streets. Each movement was a reminder of the discomfort I couldn't leave behind. My disjointed thoughts felt equally numb as if polluted water had filled my mind so completely that I couldn't see beyond the stagnant, opaque pool. The sound of my footsteps was increasingly drowned out by the endless downpour, isolating me even further from the life around me that had always seemed to belong to others. Suddenly, a movement caught my eye, and I turned to see a figure emerge from the shadows. Tattered clothing hung from his gaunt frame, like battle-torn flags, ragged and flapping in the chill wind, while his eyes gleamed with a half-crazed intensity. With each step, his approach grew more aggressive; he cried out in tormented despair as his gnarled hands flailed towards me, grasping my sleeve.

"Help me," he croaked, his rasping voice choking. His matted hair framed a face that bore the scars of a life I couldn't fathom, and his gaze's piercing intensity was like he could see through my very soul.

"Sorry, I have to go," I stammered, wrenching my arm from his talon-like fingers.

Trying not to give way to panic, I just quickened my pace, the echoes of my footsteps reverberating in my ears, but I knew that he was following. With every turn I made, every alley I passed, his presence lurked behind me, growing more palpable with every passing second. I felt like helpless prey, trapped in an invisible web spun by this deranged stranger. As I rounded a dimly lit corner, my heart hammered in my chest with such force that it drowned out every other noise. The heavy air filled my desperate lungs with fear until it felt like being slowly suffocated when I dared to steal a glance behind me. But he was relentless, his eyes still fixed on me with what felt like a malevolence that froze my core. Another shiver ran down my spine, and even though there was some distance between us, I felt the weight of his unwieldy frame pressing against me. At that moment, I sprinted down the nearest crowded street as the growing terror surged through my veins, fuelling my desperate escape. I could hear his laboured breathing and the irregular thud of his footsteps, drawing closer with each passing second. Adrenaline coursed through me, my survival instincts taking over as I pushed myself beyond the limits of what I might have believed was possible.

With every nerve frantically racing around my body in a rush of uncontrolled electrical impulses, I rushed towards the nearest house, going against everything that had brought me here as I was now determined to stay alive. With trembling hands, I desperately pounded on the door, praying that someone would answer while being acutely aware that the uneven, shuffling footsteps behind me were getting closer. At last, the door swung open, revealing a darkened hallway. Without hesitation, I darted inside, my breath hitching in my throat. The door clattered behind me, shutting out the threatening darkness and the wailing man, who cursed loudly before half-falling down the few wooden steps and stumbling back to the street. I didn't move until the only sound was the merciless rain and my shallow breathing. Trembling and shaken, I wondered how he had become so tormented that his reality was now terrifying. But I knew the question was pointless; I could do nothing for him. Aside from anything else, I was certainly in no position to judge anyone; I'd been trapped in a crippling waltz with my own demons for what felt like forever. So, for now, it had to be enough that I was safe.

Even though my body was still quivering with raw anxiety, I slowly walked along the hallway, which led to a small sitting room.

When I was sure the house was empty, I settled onto the worn, threadbare couch, and a wholly unexpected sense of relief gently overcame me, like a soft breeze whispering through the cracks of my fractured mind. The abandoned house creaked and groaned as dust particles danced in the slivers of light that pierced through the tattered curtains, casting slashes of neon across the well-worn carpet. With each breath, my once-frantic heartbeat slowed, finding strange comfort in this seemingly forgotten place. The musty scent of nostalgia mingled with the rain-soaked air as I closed my eyes and found peace in the silence, intentionally freeing my mind, even if it would only be for a fleeting moment.

Wrapped in the embrace of an old, moth-eaten blanket, I nestled deeper into the worn cushions of the dilapidated couch. The pitter-patter of rain against the window provided a rhythmic backdrop to the omnipresent swirl of troubled thoughts. My mind traced back through a maze of memories; the weight of my past mistakes bore down upon me, and all the regrets scratched deep into the fragile fabric of my being.

I pondered every choice that had brought me to this point. But now, after suddenly being so desperate to survive, the question was, had I wanted to kill myself at all? What if all those intensely painful thoughts that haunted every waking moment weren't portraying reality and were nothing more than my mind's spiteful, malicious creations? I anxiously glanced around me. And what was I even doing here? Almost nesting, putting effort into finding comfort rather than just ending it, away from the harsh gaze of the world that held nothing for me. And perhaps most troubling of all, had those therapists been right? Could it be that we might find the strength to rise again in the depths of our lowest moments? I shook my head to dislodge this last question; it was far too uncomfortable to contemplate, even for a moment, that it could be true.

I wandered into the neglected kitchen, my footsteps leaving imprints on the grimy linoleum floor. Drawers scraped open as I rummaged through them, hoping to find some sustenance amidst the remnants of someone else's life. My hand brushed against a small package, and I felt a glimmer of hope. I hastily unwrapped the brittle biscuits, their stale aroma mingling with the scent of abandonment. Returning to the couch, I settled once more to eat, soon finding yet more comfort in each crumbling mouthful. After savouring the last piece, I shifted position and felt something under my folded legs.

Curiosity got the better of me, so I tentatively reached down and felt my fingers touch something hidden beneath a worn cushion. After a gentle tug, I pulled out what seemed to be some kind of notebook that had become worn over time as the delicate pages were distinctly yellowed. As I carefully opened it, the scent of aged paper blended seamlessly with the musty air. Words, handwritten in elegant cursive, were faded yet still legible, danced before my eyes as if excitedly inviting me to read them and unravel their secrets. Tracing my fingers over the almost bleached ink, I could sense a voice, no more than a distant echo, that had been silent for many years and was now trying to speak to me. For no logical reason, it felt as if there was something within these pages that held some kind of promise. So, despite all my perfectly reasonable doubts, the disbelief was firmly silenced, and I chose to read. With the notebook nestled in my lap, I inched over to get the full benefit of a small pool of pale yellow light from the street outside. Once comfortable, I opened the book to the first page, determined I could ignore the heaviness of my weary body and the endless clamour of my thoughts. However, sheer exhaustion took hold, leaving me to read no more than the first line.

Startled from sleep, my eyes widened in surprise as I met the gaze of an old lady sitting in the armchair before me. Her presence radiated a timeless elegance, her floral dress a delicate tapestry of colours that whispered tales of long-forgotten summers. By her side rested a large, black leather handbag with a brass clasp, the shoulder strap folded in a neat coil. With her hair perfectly styled and smart silver-buckled shoes, she exuded an air of grace that calmly defied her shabby surroundings. Her eyes, wise and knowing, held a glimmer of warmth as she looked at me with a gentle smile. Her pearl white teeth were framed by perfectly applied lipstick that glowed with the deep pinkish orange of a sunset. I awkwardly sat up, stumbling over my words, my voice barely a whisper as I greeted this unexpected visitor, clumsily apologising for being in what I assumed was her home.

With a serene poise, the older woman raised a hand, her dulcet voice floating through the room like a melodic prayer.

"My child," she said, her voice carrying the weight of wisdom and compassion, "there is no intrusion." Her words wrapped around me like a comforting embrace, dissolving the tension that had surreptitiously invaded my bones.

"You are simply looking for the peace that I have always found here," she continued, her eyes filled with understanding. "I know you feel broken, but even though some pieces seem to be lost forever, I promise you, they are simply waiting to be rediscovered."

Like the flutter of butterfly wings, her words landed softly on me. In the presence of this enigmatic soul, I started to feel a strange sense of belonging, as if some unknown force had conspired to bring us together.

"I should have said earlier," I began hesitantly, "my name is Jenna, Jenna Howard."

The woman nodded but didn't immediately respond, so as politely as possible, I asked what I should call her.

"I am Athena May Bower," she announced slowly, relishing every syllable as if her mouth were enjoying fine wine's rich taste.

"It's a pleasure to meet you, Ms. Bower," I answered, her expression showing her distinct pleasure at my respectful tone.

"You may call me Miss Athena May," she replied graciously, "that will do nicely."

As she spoke, her gaze shifted to the worn notebook beside me. Her eyes sparkled with delight, with a distinct hint of nostalgia dancing within their depths.

"I see you've discovered my journal," she remarked, her voice tinged with a mixture of fondness and anticipation.

"It holds so much, a treasure trove of experiences."

She paused and looked at me intently as if trying to discern whether I would answer truthfully.

"Have you read any of my work?"

When I quickly explained that had been my intention, but I had fallen asleep before really getting much further than the first few lines, she smiled knowingly.

"Would you like to read some now?"

Intrigued by her offer, I nodded, and she gestured for me to pull a small velvet-cushioned stool closer to her chair, patiently waiting until I was settled. When she was satisfied I was comfortable, she indicated it was time for me to peel back the cover.

At first, as I carefully turned page after page, the woman's eyes shimmered with recognition. She nodded toward a particular entry, her voice carrying a sense of reverence.

"Ah, so many memories," she whispered, her voice trembling with emotion.

With bated breath, I listened as she started to reveal how so much of her life had been captured on those delicate pages. "It began as nothing more than a way of remembering," she said quietly, "but it gained more significance for me as time passed. I suppose to those who might give it no more than a cursory glance, it's nothing more than a personal record of a journey. But, if you look a little deeper, like most lives, it's a love story."

Suddenly, this brief visit to her past became too much for her to bear as I noticed tears glistening in the corners of her eyes.

"Thank you for finding this for me; it is overwhelming to be in the company of these precious recollections again," she murmured, her voice filled with gratitude.

Together, we sat there, enveloped in a comforting silence, until after several minutes, Athena May spoke again, "You know, child, the past not only shapes us but also has the power to heal, to mend the fragments of our souls, and to remind us that, despite the passage of time, our stories will always endure." She stopped and looked at me with an unwavering gaze, "Everyone matters, not only because of where we are from, although that should never be forgotten. But also, and in some ways, more importantly, where we are going."

I swallowed hard, knowing that even though I had said almost nothing about myself, she somehow knew of my ongoing struggle and maybe even the decision I had reached about my life.

As the first rays of the rising sun painted the room in warm shades, the older woman's voice grew softer.

"Jenna, my child, it is time for me to go," she whispered, "but you can stay if you wish to, for I will come back, I promise. As sure as Summer follows Spring and every river finds its way back to the sea, we will meet again very soon."

An unexpected longing overwhelmed me as her words hung in the air. Throughout the night, I had grown accustomed to her presence; she had brought a warmth I had not experienced in such a long time. With a tender smile, she nodded towards the worn notebook still resting in my hand.

"I'll trust you with my journal and the stories it holds," she continued, "with the genuine hope you might find something within my words that will ignite some small spark of inspiration."

As she stood up, a graceful figure bathed in the soft glow of early dawn, I felt a mixture of sincere gratitude tinged with sadness.

"But for now, try and sleep; I have kept you awake long enough."

Obediently, I rested on the couch and pulled the blanket to my chin, tucking the treasured journal under a cushion. With a final nod and a slight smile of approval, Athena May turned to leave, pausing to pick up the handbag, and then she walked towards the dust-filled haze of the still-darkened hallway.

CHAPTER TWO

With Athena May gone, I was alone again in the abandoned house, the hushed stillness like an unseen mist. Flickering lights danced on the cracked walls, their graceful movements echoing the last of her departing footsteps. Even though I hadn't heard the front door close or a key turn in the lock, there was no question she had left the house. Suddenly, the air felt heavy with the weight of memories, and the house itself seemed to have changed as if it was now holding its breath, waiting for something. Remembering her instructions, I closed my eyes; for once, my mind had reached some kind of peace, and no thoughts disrupted my sleep.

When I awoke, I immediately found myself drawn to the old notebook. For a moment of trepidation and curiosity, I allowed my fingers to idle on the faded spine and feel the hushed murmurs of forgotten stories beneath my touch. As I opened the pages, a soft sigh seemed to escape from within while the house exhaled with relief. I did not doubt that every word, each ink stroke, held the imprint of a life once lived. As I began to read, I quickly became lost in the chorus of once-silenced voices that started to fill the abandoned rooms.

I shall begin at the beginning...

The deep golden sun rose slowly over the endless fields every morning, casting long shadows across the ramshackle house where I grew up. It was a humble place, where the flaked paint on the walls and the weathered floorboards echoed with the presence of all those who had lived there before. It provided little warmth in the chill of Winter but could become stifling in the Summer, particularly on my mother's baking days. The air would be dry and hot, filled with clouds of floating flour grains that drifted like fine snow, as she kneaded the dough on the roughly hewn wooden table my father had made. Too often, we would complain about the heat, but only until the heady aroma of fresh bread surrounded us, our stomachs would rumble, and all thought turned from the discomfort of the soaring temperatures to the delicious prospect of stuffing ourselves with doorstep-sized slices slathered with heavily-scented homemade jam.

To even the most casual onlooker, it would have been obvious that my family lived a life of poverty, scraping by on what little we had. But despite all the struggles, our united determination was always coupled with an unshakeable hope that things would get better. My mother worked tirelessly to put food on the table; when not in the field, she walked miles to help our neighbours. She had a rare knowledge of plants and herbs, which, with skills learned from my grandmother, she could combine and make natural medicines. While my father spent every day either working with the animals or caring for our meagre crops, his calloused hands were a testament to his unwavering dedication to his family.

Growing up in such circumstances was undeniably challenging, although I didn't appreciate it as much at the time. I see now there was something unexpectedly beautiful in its simplicity. The melodic chirruping of the crickets at night, the sugary-sweet smell of honeysuckle on warm Summer days and magical nights spent gazing up at the twinkling stars in the deep blue, velvet sky it was always these things that brought boundless joy to our lives.

Looking back on those days, I realise they ultimately shaped who I became as a woman. They taught me the value of hard work, perseverance, and the importance of family. And though we may have been poor, what mattered was that we were rich in spirit and abundant in love.

One day, a generous neighbour gave me a book. It was a thin volume with a tattered cover, but to me, it was a rare treasure. I had never had a book of my own before, and simply holding it in my hands filled me with a sense of

*wonder. My younger sister, Ellie, pestered me to see it, but
I resisted. Her hands were always either covered in soil
from her attempts at gardening or, worse still, stained with
berry juice. So, to appease her, I gave her my prized rag
doll, Maryanne, and then retreated to the quiet solitude of
my room and read.*

*I had been introduced to literature from an early age as
our family's prized possession was a leather-bound Bible,
which lived on the high shelf in my parents' bedroom. Even
though they were relatively easygoing, touching the book
without them was absolutely forbidden. So when my father
lifted it down to read, Ellie and I would instantly take our
places on either side of him and wonder at the printed
words and illuminated colour plates depicting pivotal
moments within the story. His deep voice gave every verse
so much meaning and was said with such reverence that
even though we didn't always understand the significance,
we instinctively knew it was important. Even Ellie, who
usually chatted away incessantly like a baby bird crying
out for food from its mother, stayed silent. The only sound
besides my father's voice was the rhythmic creaking of my
mother's rocking chair, punctuated by the soft click of her
knitting needles. These evenings happened regularly, so it
was probably inevitable that when I was no more than five*

or six, we all became acutely aware that I could read on my own.

So, when I received that first book, the words on the page danced before my eyes, introducing me to a world of characters who lived in places I had never been. It's true; the actual story was simple, but it spoke to me in a way that nothing ever had before. I practically devoured the pages for hours, losing myself in its world. When I finally came out of my room, it was with a newfound sense of purpose. I wanted to read more, to learn more, to experience more. And so, I began seeking books wherever they could be found. At first, I begged for cast-off volumes from friends and neighbours, but seeing the intense embarrassment this caused my parents, I began doing any paid work and saved my meagre wage to give to my father. So, when he went into town, he could buy another book from the second-hand store. Very often, their condition was poor; covers were torn, or there was untidy, scrawling handwriting in every page margin. But I didn't care, and on witnessing my devotion, my mother gave me an old sewing box so I could store my collection away from Ellie's grasping fingers.

I know, without question, that the first book was a turning point in my life. It opened the door to a world of endless possibilities that I have continued exploring ever since. And though I may have started life in poverty, with nothing but the love of my family and the magic of books, I knew that if I always tried my hardest, I could probably do anything. With each passing day, my dream to explore the world beyond my family home only grew stronger. And so, one day, when my best friend, Cassie, invited me to visit the nearby town, I jumped at the opportunity. After much pleading with my parents, they finally relented, having extracted the promise I would be back before nightfall. Just the journey to the town was an adventure, as we had yet to be anywhere without at least one adult. We walked along between the fields of golden wheat that swayed in the breeze as if an unseen hand was sweeping over the outstretched stems, causing them to rhythmically bend in soft waves. With each step, showers of pale-yellow dust rose from our ill-fitting buckled shoes that had been handed down from others. Although they pinched, we were grateful for the welcome protection against the sharp stones that littered the path. Even though it was still early, the sun was already baking the earth, and so, for as much as possible, we stayed under the protective shade of the towering trees that lined the road. The air was alive with the joyous trilling of birds and the endless hum of insect wings as they flew amongst the rich foliage, and the honeyed scent of wildflowers filled my nostrils.

When we finally arrived at the town, I was immediately struck by its sights and sounds. People bustled about, going about their daily business. Unlike the rough paths of home, these streets were paved with smooth stones. Vast buildings rose high into the sky, their windows glittering in the sunlight. With each step, I felt more and more like Dorothy discovering the world of Oz, with everything around me feeling both strange and magical as it was all so unlike home.

We wandered through the crowded streets, taking in everything around us. We visited the market, where vendors sold fruits, vegetables, spices, and sweets piled high on wheeled carts. We saw a band of musicians performing, their harmonies filling the air while the audience swayed and clapped in time. Finally, we overcame our shyness and joined them, and with each song, our enthusiasm increased until we were dancing and twirling, oblivious to the mild amusement of those around us. Then we stopped at a small lemonade stand, where we sipped from tiny paper cups and watched the world go by, perched on the kerbside.

*With the sun slowly sinking behind the distant trees, we
slowly made our way back home, both too tired to talk
much. In the few words we exchanged, there was no
question Cassie preferred our life in the country. It felt
safe, whereas to her, the town was just too loud, too filled
with strangers, and you couldn't even see what was around
the next corner. But there wasn't a doubt that I had a very
different opinion. I knew that my life would always be
rooted in the countryside, and I was very proud of my
family. But now I had seen with my own eyes that there was
more to life. Despite all those books, there was far more in
the world than I could ever have imagined.*

*But another day was of even greater significance, which
began when the sun's golden rays had only just started to
paint the horizon, announcing that the time had finally
come when I could start school. Ellie complained
vociferously that I was allowed to do something that she
could not but was soon pacified by my mother, who wearily
promised they could bake together. After listening again to
my father remind me of the importance of education and
never forgetting to respect my teacher, I was finally
allowed to leave the house. As I set off, clutching my
carefully prepared lunch bag, it felt like the crisp air was
carrying whispers of possibility and adventure. With each*

*step, anticipation danced within my heart, for today held
the promise of discovery.*

*As soon as I walked through the red-painted doors, the
scent of books mingled with the fragrance of freshly
sharpened pencils. The air was filled with the excited
chatter of my classmates, and I quickly took my place at a
small wooden desk that I was to share with Cassie. We
gazed around the small room. Colourful posters adorned
the walls on which shelves had been fixed that groaned
under the weight of art supplies and crisp towers of pristine
white paper. For others in that room, it might not have
seemed exciting at all, but for me, it was like I had entered
Aladdin's cave. Amid that enchantment, there was a
teacher whose passion for literature radiated like a beacon
in the night. Mrs. Jenkins possessed a spirit that effortlessly
transcended the confines of the classroom. With each word
she spoke, we were transported to faraway places as she
unveiled the beauty hidden within the pages of books. Her
voice, soft yet commanding, held an allure that captivated
even the most restless students. Her classroom became a
sacred space where imagination flourished, and minds
were expanded.*

*Mrs Jenkins would gather us around like a circle of eager
disciples, her eyes twinkling with anticipation. With*

reverence, despite our young age, she would share tales of
literary giants, their words dancing upon her lips.
Shakespeare and Austen were two of her many favourites,
but for me, it was Charles Dickens. Over time, his
characters would become my friends; their struggles
seemed very like my own, and when she read passages from
'Oliver Twist', I was nothing less than spellbound.
One hot afternoon, she instructed us to line up in pairs and
informed the class that we were going on a trip to the other
school building much larger than our own. It was where
the older children attended and was at most half a mile
away. Showing incredible patience, she herded us along the
dusty path, gently admonishing anyone who straggled
behind the leading group. As always, Cassie and I had been
partnered together, and all the way, we excitedly
speculated on the purpose of this excursion. When we
arrived, Mrs Jenkins reminded us that lessons were still in
session, so it was essential to be quiet. Dutifully, the class
followed her into the building like a row of wide-eyed,
anxious ducklings desperate to stay close to their mother.
We hurried along a long corridor until we reached an
impressive wooden door with a large brass handle that
glowed like pure gold against the weathered oak. Before
Mrs Jenkins even had time to speak, my young eyes fell on

a shining metal plate; one word was etched into the surface- 'Library'. After being reminded again of the importance of silence, Mrs Jenkins explained that we had been given permission to visit but could only stay for a short while, so she firmly suggested we make the most of our time.

When she pushed open the door, it creaked as if to announce our arrival, and I stepped into a realm where time seemed to instantly stand still. Even though I was aware of the excited whispers of my classmates, I could say nothing as my mind tried to take in everything. Shelves upon shelves stretched out before me, adorned with treasures that spanned the ages. The scent of worn pages and ink danced in the air, whispering secrets of forgotten worlds. My fingers gently brushed against the spines, tracing the titles etched upon them as if I was trying to somehow connect with the lives contained within. With each book I carefully pulled from the shelf, it seemed a new world slowly unfurled before my eyes with every page turn. I was so lost in my thoughts that it was only when Mrs Jenkins spoke, I realised that she was standing by my side. "I knew this visit might mean the most to you, Athena May," she said quietly; without looking at her, I sighed with undiluted pleasure.

"If I lived a hundred years, I still wouldn't have time to read all these books."

She smiled and softly rested her hand on my shoulder, "Well, I don't know about a hundred years, but I have asked the librarian if you might visit here again, and she has kindly given permission. You won't be able to take any books home, but as long as you behave respectfully, you can read for a while."

My heart leapt with unfettered joy in my chest, and, for a moment, I wanted to cry out, but thankfully, I remembered the silence rule and forced myself just to smile up at her while whispering my gratitude. From that day forward, while my classmates played in the sunshine at the end of every school day, I would hurry to the library, where literary characters became my companions, their stories intertwining with my own. That building became where my imagination soared beyond the boundaries of reality. And very often, as the sun bid farewell and the early evening twilight embraced the world outside, I would reluctantly leave the library and wander home, my head filled with questions about what might happen next in any given story.

Years later, I went back to visit, and much to my surprise, what had seemed like a vast space to me as a child was

*little more than a large room. But even though I had been
wrong about its dimensions, even as an adult, there was
that same tremor of excited anticipation as I ambled
between the shelves, stopping to touch a much-loved book
that still contained my youthful joy when we had first met
all those years ago.*

*I understand now that Mrs. Jenkins taught us to read not
only with our eyes but with our hearts. Through her
guidance, literature became a tapestry of emotions, a
mirror that reflected our hopes, fears, and dreams, and her
teaching has stayed with me throughout my life, none more
so than when I began to try and write my own words.*

Knowing I needed to think, I laid down the notebook and
sat by the window, peering through the torn remnants of the
curtains, completely unseen by the world outside. The wind
whispered through the broken glass, carrying fragments of
distant conversations. I found myself wondering that, like
the young Athena May, maybe the stories within these
pages were not confined to the inked lines; perhaps they
could have some relevance to my own life. With each
passing hour, I waited, never once contemplating going
back to my own house as I knew she would return, and I
wanted to be here to welcome her.

CHAPTER THREE

As the moon cast its magical glow through the cracked windows, the abandoned house played host to strange silhouettes that flickered and waltzed on the faded walls when momentarily bathed in the harsh brightness of passing car headlights. Lost in sleep, I was awoken by a startled screech from outside; as my eyes adjusted to the darkness, I could see Athena May quietly sitting, seemingly lost in her own thoughts. The armchair cradled the old woman, her eyes filled with profound depth met my gaze with a gentle understanding. A tangible calm filled the air as if the house had summoned her back on my behalf to continue the story that had been left unfinished.

"You came back," I gasped while still rubbing the last of sleep from my eyes.

"I gave you my word, child," she replied softly, "Have you been reading my journal?"

I swung my legs excitedly over the edge of the couch, making my feet land heavily on the floor. I felt almost childlike as I talked about the rural house, the first book, the trip into town and starting school. As I spoke, Athena May sat and watched with slight amusement at my enthusiasm but said nothing until I finally paused for breath, but not before asking whether she still loved to read as much now as she had as a child. She smiled and rested back in the armchair.

"Oh yes, as you now understand, in the pages of a book, I always found an escape from the chaos of life. So, it follows, as an adult, when the outside world demands my attention, I can feel myself becoming overwhelmed. But as soon as I'm reading, I am free from it all. I love the power of a story; it's as if I'm watching a magician as the author transforms the ordinary into the extraordinary."

I edged forward; just hearing her voice was like a soothing balm, so I hoped she would understand and keep talking without me having to ask. As if hearing my unspoken plea, she closed her eyes and allowed her words to flow.

"Ah, despite everything I have done and seen, reading was always my first love. Although I love all art forms, theatre and movies, they've never failed to move me. She paused; I heard her take a deep breath, and a slight smile of satisfaction played across her lips.

"I vividly recall a day in my childhood, the first time I ever saw a movie. It felt like we were setting out on a grand adventure as my family clambered on the bus to go into the city."

Athena May must have noticed me shift forward as she continued her story, now sure of my interest.

"Ellie and I held hands so tightly as we walked slightly ahead of our parents. The heady scent of warm popcorn wafted through the air and mingled with our youthful anticipation. When we settled into those plush red seats, it was as if we were royalty sitting on plush velvet thrones. As the curtains parted and the screen came alive, my heart skipped a beat, and I felt Ellie's grip tighten to the point that my fingers almost went numb, but I didn't care at all. The audience's laughter echoed like sweet music, sending ripples of joy through my young heart. But in other parts of the story, the heartbreaking tears shed by the characters stirred emotions within me that even though I didn't entirely understand, there was no way of ignoring them."

"What happened next?" I asked, well aware I sounded childlike, but I was now so invested in the story I had long ceased to care.

"Leaving the movie theatre was bittersweet, as for all of us, it was a return to reality from the dreamlike world we had explored. On the bus home, Ellie fell asleep in my father's arms while I rested my head on my mother's shoulder. Every so often, I would glance up at her face; her eyes were misted, and I knew it was because she was remembering every moment in the film."

There was a brief silence until I asked if they had gone to the cinema regularly after that first time.

"You must remember, we did not have a lot of money, but somehow, my mother saved as much as she could. So, we would make that trip again when there was a birthday or some other special occasion. All of us were wearing our best Sunday clothes, with Ellie and me both having such huge bows in our hair. My father joked that if there was a strong breeze, the pair of us were at risk of taking off into the air like helpless birds. Mama would always scowl and only tighten those ribbons while he chuckled to himself at the image in his mind."

As a great painter with a rich palette of colour, she took something seemingly ordinary and deftly created a true masterpiece before my eager eyes. With each sentence, I started to lose myself. Time became little more than an illusion as minutes transformed into hours. With all its soul-sapping stress, the world outside faded into insignificance as her words took hold, their power seeping into the fabric of my existence. But then Athena May suddenly stopped, as if a previously unnoticed detail had suddenly made itself known.

"Come closer; I'd like to ask you a question."

With my heart racing with curiosity and reverence, I approached the armchair with cautious steps. The air crackled with the heady mixed emotions that somehow filled the space between us. I wanted her to talk more, but when we locked eyes, her expression changed from blissful to one of deep concern.

"Are you lonely, child?" she asked, her large eyes searching my face for some sign of agreement. Suddenly, I felt acutely embarrassed and looked down at the threadbare carpet like a child might do as they're being scolded. I felt uncomfortably vulnerable and wanted more than anything to firmly dismiss her assumption. But I knew in my heart to do so would be a lie, and I was also very aware that by asking the question, Athena May already knew the answer. "I have always been alone," I began, "there's only been one time when it felt like I was a part of something, that I had a place," I paused as it felt like the memory was slowly constricting my throat. After taking a deep breath, I was just able to finish the sentence,

"But that time was taken away," I shook my head, "No, that's not true," Because of me, that time was lost," I corrected myself, "Anyway, aside from then, I've never really belonged anywhere."

I stopped again and looked at her,

"Most of my life, I've felt like a spectator, stuck behind the wrong side of a glass wall, watching life happen in front of me but never being a part of it."

Athena nodded her understanding,

"It's true, child, loneliness can weigh upon a soul like a heavy stone, leaving us feeling lost and adrift. We long for the warmth of even the briefest human connection in those moments. Even just a kind word, a simple touch, or a listening ear can make all the difference. But as in many other things in life, if we look hard enough, even on those darkest days, we can learn something positive."

Despite my initial disbelief at her assertion, in the hushed stillness of the night, Athena May continued her voice with a melodic cadence that echoed within the bare room. Her words flowed like a river, effortlessly carrying me along its gentle current.

"You see, child, I can only share what I have learned; it is for you to decide whether or not it makes any sense to you. I've learned a lot about life when I have experienced loneliness. How important it is to take the time to listen to my heart and to connect with the deepest parts of myself that normally remain hidden. Do you understand?"

As I nodded and sat back on the couch, she leaned forward as if this simple movement would add more impact to her already powerful words.

"Although it wasn't always easy, I've come to understand that time spent in my own company is a gift. I have spent many days simply appreciating the incredible beauty of the world around me. And amid my loneliness, I've been reminded that we are surrounded by so much life. In those moments, I rediscovered my strength and believe, Jenna, you can do the same."

"I don't see the world as beautiful at all," I replied truthfully. As soon as I'd said the words, I felt regret as she visibly winced, as if the statement had caused her some level of physical pain.

"Oh, but it is! Yes, there is ugliness, but, for the most part, that's when people have interfered too much with the natural order of things. But if you look closely, even where lifeless concrete has been needlessly spread over the earth, you'll see plants pushing through. Often, it can be no more than a single, tiny flower. Yet despite its apparent frailty, it's filled with a fierce resilience to live, to claim its rightful place in the sun, and we can have that too."

With his last phrase, she settled back in the armchair, her steady gaze still fixed on me, as if hoping at least some of her words resonated. But I found myself unable to speak as my eyes stung with tears, and the huge lump in my throat prevented little more than a whispered sigh from escaping my mouth.

"Why are you crying?" she asked gently, "for there is no need for tears."

I swallowed hard before forcing myself to reply,

"I wasn't strong or resilient," I croaked, "Life would have been different if I had been."

Athena May shook her head,

"Don't speak of yourself in the past tense, child, for as long as you are here with me, in this house, you're in the present."

Before I had a chance to answer, she rose from the chair and, as before, collected her handbag and walked towards the hallway. Sensing my dismay, she stopped and looked back at me,

"I will return, Jenna, but while I'm away if you feel it might help, read more of my journal, and we will talk again very soon," as Athena May was about to turn away, she stopped and pointed toward the kitchen, "you must be hungry, child, there's soup on the stove and some homemade bread too, it's wrapped in the white cloth."

Without another word, she disappeared into the hallway, leaving me completely stunned, as somehow, I hadn't noticed the familiar odour of decay had been utterly overwhelmed by the rich aromas of tomato and herbs. The endless silence was now broken by a gentle bubbling sound emanating from a large stainless-steel pot, its circular lid jiggling slightly like a delicate cymbal rhythmically tapping against the rim. The effect on me was akin to the flute music played by the fabled Pied Piper; as I was drawn toward the kitchen, my senses quickly overcame my initial disbelief. I hunted through the drawers and found a solitary spoon. I lifted the lid without thinking, and the searing heat instantly radiated through my hand. Undaunted, I slipped the sleeve of my jumper over my fingers and tried again; as the heavy scent of the soup filled my nostrils, I sighed with undiluted pleasure. Gingerly, I took a small spoonful and allowed it to slip between my lips; immediately, my whole body felt warmer as the delicious liquid flowed around me as if carried by my veins. After replacing the pot lid, I ladled spoonfuls into a small bowl and eagerly sat down at the kitchen table, suddenly realising that, just as Athena May had said, there was a large loaf of bread waiting for me.

After eating almost precisely half of both the bread and soup, determined to save some for later, I returned to the couch feeling both comfortable and calm, as if somehow the old lady's words about loneliness had been ingested with the soup and were now firmly lodged in my mind, filling a space which until this moment, had been filled only with crippling doubts. With the blanket rearranged over me, I opened the notebook and settled down to read.

As I grew older, my fascination with the world beyond my home only grew stronger. Also, I felt like I'd read every book in the county and had been left frustrated. I longed for more. And so, after months of secretly studying the job advertisements in the newspaper, an opportunity finally presented itself. They were looking for clerks to work in the main post office building in the city. Not daring to believe I might secure a position; I told nobody about my application. Lord, I must have written that letter a hundred times or more until it was just right! But a week or so later, Miss Jackson from the store appeared at our front door with an official-looking letter addressed to me. Luckily, I was the only one at home, which allowed me to read before the rest of my family returned at the end of the day.

I could hardly believe my eyes when I saw the words, I had been accepted on a trial basis; my heart leapt with joy. But my euphoria was short-lived when I realised there could be no delay in telling my parents. We sat down after dinner, and then I showed them the letter. My mother sat in silence as my father read aloud and then turned to me.

"Are you sure you're ready to go?" he asked solemnly; when I nodded my response, he sighed heavily.

"Then you must, but only on the condition you never forget your home and if things don't work out, you come back."

"I promise," I answered, hardly daring to look at my mother as I could see she was dabbing her eyes with the small lace handkerchief she kept in her apron pocket. As for Ellie, she only asked if she could have the bigger bed now, I was going!

Leaving my family and the only home I had ever known was both daunting and exhilarating. When the day came, I packed the small leather suitcase my mother had bought from a thrift store. After repeating the promise to my father, he pressed some money into my hand.

"It's not much Athena May but try and keep it for emergencies."

The journey to the city was long and draining. I had to take the bus, and as I gazed at the ever-changing landscape, I

*alternated between feeling incredibly homesick and
breathlessly excited. But the anticipation of the unknown
kept me going. When I finally arrived, my weariness was
easily overcome by the sheer joy of taking that first step.
The childlike excitement of that first visit to town was
nothing compared to seeing the city. It was extraordinary,
filled with towering skyscrapers that gleamed on either side
of the crowded streets, overloading my senses with
intensely bright lights and near-constant noise. People with
determined expressions rushed about, their hurried
footsteps like a rhythmic drumbeat on the pavement. The
air was thick with the scent of exhaust fumes, the deafening
sound of blaring car horns and irate taxi drivers yelling
expletives when held back by blinking traffic lights.
In those first weeks, more than once, I yearned to hear
joyous birdsong, the whispers of a breeze as it shared
timeless secrets with the long grass. To spend lazy
afternoons sprawled by the creek watching iridescent
dragonflies hover effortlessly over the silver-edged water
like winged ballerinas patiently waiting for their cue to
perform. In truth, everything that had always delighted my
senses and carried within the pure country air of home.
Working in the city was a whole new experience. I quickly
learned my job responsibilities, and the people I worked*

*with became like a second family to me. Eventually, I
learned to navigate the busy streets and crowded buses. I
even found time to explore the city by spending my weekend
afternoons walking through art galleries and exploring
museums. Though I missed my family and our home, the
longer I stayed in the city, I knew this decision was right.
The opportunities seemed endless, and I felt as though I
was truly living for the first time in my life. Without fail, I
wrote to my parents every week, sometimes including
postcards of the places I had visited for Ellie. My mother
took it upon herself to reply; her letters were filled with
stories of our neighbours and new recipes she had tried,
but always ended with a sincere hope that I was looking
after myself and was genuinely happy. Studying her careful
prose made me homesick every time; I found myself resting
my fingertips on the pages as if, in some way, I could
connect with her. Touching where she had touched.
Although there were often tears, my belief that I was on the
right path remained unshakeable, even after a particularly
disturbing encounter.*

*It happened on what I can only describe as a solemn
evening, as the air felt heavy, as if carrying the weight of
an impending storm. I felt unsettled. With every hurried
step, my breathing became shallower, and the welcoming*

familiarity of the streets near my home now seemed filled
with unexplainable apprehension.

As I turned a corner, I felt the presence of a hunched figure
lurking in an abandoned shop doorway. A cold shiver
raced down my spine like I'd been doused in freezing
water, and every sense instantly heightened. Suddenly,
lurching from darkness stood an angry young man, his face
etched with fearful determination, and in his hand, I saw
the glint of a knife blade. For a moment, I could feel the
paralysis of fear starting to creep into my body, but
somehow, and to this day, I have no idea where it came
from; I found the strength to defy the mugger's intentions.
Not by taking any kind of physical action, as there was no
question I could not compete, so instead, I spoke to him.
Even though my voice was trembling, my show of apparent
defiance seemed to take him by total surprise as I noticed
his hand drop. I cannot claim to have said anything
especially wise or profound; I simply asked why he wanted
to attack me, as surely it was obvious, I had nothing of any
great value. For a brief moment, our eyes met. It seemed as
if my words resonated with him, so I just talked more about
how I earned relatively little and the few pieces of jewellery
I was wearing, although priceless to me, were of little
monetary value. Suddenly, without speaking a word, he

turned and ran down an alleyway. I watched as he leapt,
with extraordinary athleticism, over the wire fence and
disappeared back into the shadows. When I was sure he
had gone, I raced home, my heart frantically beating
against my ribs like a hummingbird's wings, only stopping
to breathe when I had locked my front door behind me.
But after a day or two, I realised that the encounter, though
marked by danger, could transform my perception of the
world and taught me a valuable lesson. It proved, beyond
doubt, that strength is not the absence of fear but the
audacity to defy it. So, from that day forward, I knew I
could walk down any street in the world and not be scared
of what might happen.
One of the infinitely happier highlights of my first month in
the city came when I received my first wages. Although
nothing unusual in the grand scheme of things, it was a
moment of great personal pride. I remember holding that
paycheck in my hand, relishing the feel of the crisp paper
and filled with a real sense of accomplishment. For now, I
had tangible proof that my efforts had been appreciated.
My heart swelled when, for the first time, I deposited money
into my newly opened bank account, knowing that I had
earned every penny. It was a moment of empowerment, but
more than anything, it represented a sense of

independence. I was no longer reliant on anyone else for my financial well-being. I could support myself, to make my own choices, and pursue all my dreams.

One evening, after a long day at work, some of my coworkers suggested we go to a small nightclub in the city. I had never been anywhere like it before. Still, I was so eager for every new experience that I put aside my trepidation and readily accepted. And so, we made our way to the club, the sound of a lively jazz band like a clarion call, growing louder with each step we took.

Once inside, it was small and dimly lit, the air thick with the heady combination of sweat and alcohol. The dance floor was heaving with people, their bodies moving in perfect harmony with the rhythm of the music. The walls were adorned with low-level lights, masked with heavily fringed shades and one mirrored ball hung from the low ceiling, casting a kaleidoscope of colours across the room. We took a small table. Joe ordered drinks for us all, for which I was genuinely grateful He was a powerfully built but incredibly gentle man who supervised our office with such a calm and respectful demeanour; he was very well-liked by us all. So, in this unfamiliar place, his knowledge was most welcome as not only had I never been in such a place before. I had never drunk alcohol either, but I was curious to see what it was like. I took a sip of the drink in front of me; it was deep pink and slightly sparkling, the taste both sweet and bitter on my tongue. I knew my parents, particularly my mother, would be horrified to learn where I was and what I was doing. Still, the drive to try everything was too strong within me.

As the night wore on, I found myself feeling more and more lightheaded, the music and the alcohol blending in a dizzying haze. I stumbled onto the dance floor, my body happily trapped within the flow of the swaying crowd, my senses buzzing with the energy of the night. And though I knew that I would probably pay for my indulgence in the morning, I couldn't help but just allow it all to wash over me.

As the night came to a close and we tripped out of the club, we laughed so hard, holding each other for support as we wandered home. Joe walked with me, even offering his arm, which I gratefully took as it seemed my body wasn't entirely under my control anymore. When we reached the door of my building, I thanked him and found myself boldly kissing his cheek. He smiled shyly and walked away, but only when he was sure I was safely inside. As I fell into bed that night, I lay in the semi-darkness, the neon signs from outside intermittently lighting my room with garish red and purple. In that place, between being awake and asleep, it felt like everything I had believed about the city was true. It really was a place where I could be whoever I wanted to be and do whatever I wanted to do.

The next day, after work, I was walking down a busy city street with my mind still reeling from the previous night. It was late afternoon but still warm, so I sat at the park's edge and stared across the vast expanse of green. I was so lost in my thoughts that I was genuinely surprised to turn and see a man had sat down at the far end of the same bench. His face was wrinkled and lined with age; something about him briefly reminded me of my father, so I felt no reason to be anxious.

A small backpack rested on his lap, and he wore an old-fashioned, wide-brimmed hat. His eyes sparkled with a sense of adventure as he struck up a conversation with me, and I soon found myself drawn to him. He talked about his life, all the foreign countries and exotic cultures he had seen. His stories were so vivid and exciting I found myself hanging on his every word. There was no question in mind that this man had experienced the world in ways that were way beyond even my wild imagination. As we said our goodbyes and went our separate ways, I knew I would never forget meeting him. He had shown me that not only

was the world bigger than life in the country, which I
already knew, but there was even more than the city that
had become my home. In that one conversation, he inspired
me to seek out my own adventures beyond both of them.
The next day was a Saturday, and I woke up with one single
purpose: to experience something utterly new to me. So, I
decided to take a trip to the coast and see the ocean for the
first time. As I rode the bus to the beach, I could feel the
anticipation building inside me. Almost as soon as I
stepped off almost two hours later, the salty scent of the sea
filled the air, and the sound of the waves crashing against
the shore drew me like a magnet to the beach.
And then, finally, I saw it. The ocean stretched out before
me, an endless expanse of blue that seemed to go on
forever. The untamed waves, with their white caps, crashed
over the patient sand, only to withdraw before returning
with even more ferocity. I stopped only to quickly pull off
my shoes, knowing it would never be enough just to see it; I
had to feel it, too. I stood there, transfixed, as the water
rushed up to my feet to greet me, the chill of it sending
shivers down my spine. Perhaps for the first time in my life,
I felt truly connected to something so vast and powerful
that it took my breath away. I gazed out, while seagulls
glided effortlessly in large circles overhead, lazily

*spiralling higher and higher, leaving me to imagine what
was over the horizon.*

*I carefully negotiated my way over the slippery rocks as I
explored the beach. I found creatures and plants I had
never seen before in the myriad of tidal pools that had
briefly captured them. The sand was dotted with
translucent pink seashells, smooth pebbles and long
emerald, green ribbons of rippled seaweed, each offering a
tantalising glimpse of what existed beneath the water's
surface. As the sun began to set, I sat on a large flat rock
and watched as the sky turned from blue to orange to pink.
The colours were vibrant and alive, and even though I had
to run barefoot back to the bus stop, I wouldn't have missed
seeing them. Throughout the journey home, the sound of
the ocean rang in my ears, and my skin tingled with the
remembered warmth of the sun.*

*But only a month or so later, a new kind of adventure came
into my life at the onset of the most challenging week at my
work so far. Our beloved supervisor, Joe, was promoted,
and although I was delighted to be a part of his
celebrations, I couldn't help but feel a pang of sadness.
Since my first day, I witnessed him being a kind and
compassionate boss who has always made time to listen
and be supportive. Never once raised his voice or acted in*

any way that could make any of us feel demeaned or our efforts unappreciated. With him moving on, we all began to speculate as to who might assume his position. When someone suggested I should apply, at first, I had been reluctant, but hearing the positive encouragement, I opted to craft my application. When I was called to the upper floor, which housed all the senior staff, I admit to feeling nervous yet excited. However, these emotions remained with me for less than a few minutes when a particularly obnoxious young man took my letter, smirking at the very idea that a woman would have the audacity to even think they would be suitable. I was polite at his arrogant dismissal of my worth and left the office, returning to my desk and exhibiting the dignified silence that would definitely have garnered my mother's approval.

Now, I usually try to be a calm person as I know from experience that being angry can be like having a small, erupting volcano within me. In those moments, it feels as though I am at the mercy of my own emotions, struggling to find solid ground. And yet, amid my anger, sometimes I can find some clarity and discover a tenacity that allows me to overcome even the most difficult circumstances. So, it was with this recent blow that I weathered the emotional storm. Then, once it had passed, I was left with the strong sense that even though I might never be considered for a senior role, it was important to have my voice heard.

Now, for all my mother's aspirations, it was always best to behave like, as she would say,' a lady'. Like my grandmother, she also felt very strongly about standing up for something she believed was right. Thankfully, I had inherited this from them, and when confronted by an injustice, a fierce and powerful force coursed through my veins that couldn't be halted by anything other than taking action. Over the years, I quickly learned that standing up for myself as a woman was destined to become a part of everyday life. Along with others of my sex, I experienced being told it was always best to be quiet, to be polite and to do what's asked without complaint- even when we are clearly being mistreated or undervalued. But also, like others, I knew deep down that I was worth more than that. So the next day, I went back up to that upper floor where the same man was sitting at his desk and greeted me with the same patronising tone. As was within my rights, I asked to speak to the senior manager, and reluctantly, after unnecessary huffing and puffing on his part, I finally gained access to the inner office. A far more amenable fellow welcomed me, and with his patient and open encouragement, I began to speak up, to firmly demand the

respect and recognition I deserved. It wasn't easy. At first,
my voice trembled with uncertainty while my mind wrestled
with feelings of being afraid, vulnerable, and very alone.
On the way to this very office, I had been acutely aware I
may well face ridicule, rejection, and even hostility. But I
knew that I had to stay true to myself and my values, no
matter what.

When I felt there was nothing left to say, he smiled kindly
and commented on the eloquence of my presentation. For a
moment, I was sure he would simply thank me for my time
but do nothing more. But much to my surprise, he offered
me the role of supervisor, again on a trial basis and went
as far as assuring me, should I face any obstacles, that his
door was always open to me. The smug assistant did not
attempt to disguise his dismay at this turn of events but still
found it within himself to assure his boss the necessary
paperwork would be prepared as soon as possible.

I walked back down the stairs and had to pause more than
once as my heart was pounding wildly, and my legs felt
they could no longer bear my weight as they had turned
into the consistency of melted ice cream. Just before
returning to my desk, I silently thanked my mother and
grandmother for instilling this sense of purpose and self-

worth; it proved to be more valuable to me than any
material gift.

I wanted to read more, but my eyes stubbornly refused to stay open. So reluctantly, I closed the notebook and placed it back on the worn cushion that had become its resting place. I pulled the blanket to my chin and waited with weary anticipation for my darkest thoughts to crowd out any slight hint of light, but surprisingly, they did not appear. Instead, my mind started to fill with long-forgotten images of my own trips to the beach. They had been buried for so long, remembering them was like greeting old friends and, for the first time in what felt like forever, I began to feel almost joyful. Recollections eagerly tumbled over each other, excitedly urging me to relive them with such intensity I could practically feel the sand between my toes. The pleasure was so intense that even though I knew this feeling wasn't real and probably couldn't last, I surrendered to it anyway; I had waited too long for it to come back.

CHAPTER FOUR

A strange bumping sound from inside the house rudely brought me out of sleep. Still half-dazed, I looked around the room, expecting to see Athena May sitting in her armchair, but there was no sign of her. Feeling slightly unnerved, I threw off the blanket and rose unsteadily to my feet; as I moved, there was a distinct gasp from the doorway to the hallway. I spun around and saw a small girl, no more than nine or ten, peeking at me from around the doorframe. Only the top half of her face was visible, but her bright eyes sparkled with mischievous curiosity.

"Hello," I said quietly, not making any movement towards her, "are you alright?"

She nodded and took a couple of tentative steps into the room. She was dressed in a plaid dress with a bright blue bow at the collar, her ankle socks gleaming almost snow white in stark contrast to her black strapped shoes.

"I was looking for Miss Athena May," she explained, "I thought she came here."

Still anxious not to frighten my young visitor, I remained still.

"She's not here right now," I explained, "but she is due to come back. Can I give her a message?"

The little girl shook her head, causing her two tightly bound plaits to sway against her round cheeks.

"She's never where she should be; every time I need her, she's always somewhere else," the child pouted before seeming to remember I was there, "No, thank you," she continued politely, "I should speak with her myself."

I nodded my understanding, and for a moment, we stood awkwardly looking at each other, neither of us sure what to do or say next. Very aware of how incredibly careful any adult had to be when in the presence of a child, I waited for her to decide what she wanted to do next. At last, she shrugged her slim shoulders and turned to leave,

"I need to go now; people will be wondering where I am," she announced firmly.

Feeling almost relieved, I readily agreed that this was an excellent idea. I watched as she took a couple of steps into the hallway before stopping,

"I forgot; I dropped my ball!"

She spun around and giggled,

"That's what woke you up."

I smiled and scanned the room but couldn't see anything, so I promised if I found it, I'd keep it safe.

"Thank you, I have others, but the rainbow one is my favourite," she paused, her face frowning with deep thought, "though it's also the one I lose the most."

"So, I'm looking for a rainbow ball? I won't forget," I replied, "Oh, as for Miss Athena May, who shall I say called?"

She chuckled at my formality and half-skipped towards the door again, calling over her shoulder.

"Just say it was Miss Elizabeth, bye now."

After hearing a couple of her light footsteps on the wooden floorboards, I finally moved just to make sure she was tall enough to open the front door. But as I glanced down the hallway, it was immediately apparent she had already gone. I returned to the couch and lifted the blanket; in my haste, it had fallen onto the dusty floor. As I shook it, a small rainbow ball suddenly rolled out from under the sofa and rested at my feet. I carefully picked it up and placed it on the cushion, knowing it would be safe there until Athena May returned and I could ask how to return it to the rightful owner.

For a few moments, I was profoundly aware that I had no real idea how long I had been in the house, drifting in and out of sleep; it was almost impossible to keep track. But this thought didn't stay with me for long; after all, there was nobody who would be out looking for me, and I was in no rush to go back to my own house. Despite its comfortable size, for so long, it had felt as if the walls were alive, moving ever closer to me with every passing hour, slowly cutting off any possible way out. Too often, it felt like there wasn't even enough oxygen in the air, as the lifeless atmosphere could become stiflingly oppressive. But just as it seemed I was on the point of being overwhelmed by remembered pain, I quickly opened the notebook, knowing I could escape within its pages.

Weeks after my trip to the coast, I found myself wandering through the winding streets of the older parts of the city. Compared to the gleaming skyscrapers and traffic-choked streets where I spent most of my days, it was far quieter and blessed with the dignified elegance of age. As I walked along one particular tree-lined road, the buildings around me felt ancient and audaciously grand. Walls decorated with detailed carvings, laced with intertwining stems of dark-leaved ivy and topped by stone-carved gargoyles with soulless yet ever-watchful eyes. Wrought iron gates, often guarded by fierce creatures, deterred any stranger from contemplating going inside. I stopped and gazed through the bars, marvelling at the clipped lawns and artfully

designed topiary that often lined a tiled pathway leading to
a vast oak front door. Despite having spent some
considerable time in the city, when I stood there, I was
every inch a country girl again. Glimpsing a world that had
only ever existed in those fairytales I had devoured as a
child.

But then, as if that wasn't enough, as I turned a corner, I
saw it. Rising before me was a towering cathedral, its
elegant spires reaching towards the sky, like highly
decorated gothic fingers straining to touch the hem of
heaven. The building was awe-inspiring, a monument to the
faith and dedication of those who had built it centuries
before. As I stepped inside, I was instantly struck by the
sheer scale that left me momentarily breathless. The richly
painted ceiling seemed to soar towards infinity, its vaults
and arches creating a sense of grandeur and majesty.
The stained-glass windows were a kaleidoscope of colours,
casting vivid light patterns across the cool, marbled floor.
As I looked closer, I recognised some of the scenes so
perfectly recreated by master craftsmen; they were similar
in content to those illustrated plates within our family Bible
back home. The air was filled with the sweet scent of
incense, and the thick stone walls created a deep sense of
solemnity and peace. As I continued wandering, my shoes

clicking on the decorative tiles, it felt like I had stepped back in time. The echoes of centuries of worship seemed to fill the air. I could almost imagine the hundreds of believers who had entered this extraordinary building, hoping to find comfort and guidance. To them, like the current parishioners, it was so much more than just a monument to the past. As I left the cathedral and returned to my part of the city, despite the bustling streets, I knew that sacred space had left an indelible mark on my memory. No more than a month after I had visited the cathedral, I received some devastating news. My grandmother, who had been such an influential presence in my family's life, had passed away. I had been named after her, which was a constant source of pride for us both. As I sat in my room, tears streaming down my face, memories of her flooded my mind. I thought of the countless times she had held me close and whispered words of comfort in the warm and loving home she had always provided.

I pictured Ellie and me walking to her home in the valley, swinging the straw basket filled with baked gifts that my mother had lovingly created. On the way back home, that basket would be twice as heavy, and I'd have to urge my reluctant little sister to help me carry it. Grandma always filled it to the brim with swatches of material for Mama to

make our clothes, often a home-baked ham wrapped in
linen and, best of all, two small bags of sweets for us as
well as at least two glass jars of honey, made by her own
bees. We would stand at a safe distance while she put a fine
mesh net over her head and approached the two hives,
talking softly to the bees that flew around her like tiny,
winged planets orbiting a benevolent and gentle sun.
And then, as I sat in my small city apartment, feeling
almost lost in grief, I began to remember the stories she
had told us about her childhood over the years. Ellie and I
would sit transfixed, our mouths filled with perfect cubes of
her homemade fudge, as she shared her recollections,
which nearly always had a moral attached or a lesson to
learn. She would look at us both and solemnly make us
promise we would be wiser or more careful than she had
been. We always agreed, both of us knowing it was a pie
crust promise 'easily made, easily broken,' and by the
smile that broke on Grandma's face, she knew it too. Such
a simple memory but undeniably precious because even as
I mourned her loss, I felt so thankful for the time we had
spent together.
It wasn't long before I found myself travelling back home
for her funeral. I'd been wise enough to not only save the
emergency fund my father had given me but had managed

to add more so I could easily afford the trip. It was the first time I had been able to return since my move to the city. Under any other circumstances, I would have been excited to see my family again, but I knew the depth of sadness that would inevitably cloud this particular visit.

As I stared blankly out of the bus window, the landscape steadily changed until no more buildings blocked the view. The countryside was even more beautiful than I remembered, with rolling hills covered in a dense blanket of wildflowers stretching out as far as the eye could see. Waving fields of corn greeted me as the wind rippled through the laden stems. When we took a brief stop, like the other passengers, I got off the bus to stretch my legs. The air was cool and fresh, carrying with it the heavy aromas of pine and earth, the scent of home.

After being repeatedly hugged by my parents and even Ellie, we walked together to my grandmother's house. It was exactly as I had remembered; as we drew closer, I could almost picture her standing on the porch, waiting for us to arrive, that broad smile lighting her face, chasing away any sign of age. My mother busied herself with tidying the already immaculate home, but none of us commented; we knew it was her way of doing one last thing for her mother. When she was satisfied, we moved on to the small church where the funeral would be held. The building was aged, but its simple beauty was striking, especially the small carved cross that stood proudly on the red-tiled roof. Inside, the wooden pews were worn and polished by years of use, and the solitary stained-glass window cast a soft glow over the organ that stood to one side of the slightly raised altar.

As I sat there in the quiet of the church, listening to the prayers and Bible readings, I felt a sense of peace wash over me. The love and kindness that my grandmother had always shown filled the air, and as the congregation sang her favourite hymns, voices ringing with faith, I knew she could hear us and was smiling still. After the service, we gathered together at my parent's home for a shared meal. The table almost groaned under the weight of all the dishes that my grandmother had always cooked and more that had been brought by her neighbours and friends. Far from being a solemn occasion, the sounds of laughter and shared memories soon rang out across the fields- a true celebration of a life well lived.

As the day drew to a close, I knew that I would never forget this final journey to my grandmother's home. I watched all the guests leave, and soon, we were left alone to share our thoughts. Although we had differing opinions on many things, it was easy to agree on the power of family and the enduring spirit of those we love. My father stood up and took a few paces before turning back to face us and pulled a folded sheet of lavender notepaper from his pocket.

"I'd like to read this to you now; Grandma Athena May wrote it when she knew her time was coming.." he paused and looked at my mother, "She gave it to me for you, but I'd like to share it with our girls if that's alright."

My mother nodded, and even though there was a slight smile on her lips, I could see her eyes were already welling with tears. He cleared his throat and began to read.

"As the days slowly pass by, the world around us undergoes a constant transformation. The once-vibrant landscape of Summer gives way to the subdued and muted hues of Autumn. The trees, which were blessed with lush foliage, now shed their leaves, creating a magnificent tapestry of colours on the ground below. So, we have to always remember, although it can feel as if much is lost, especially during the harsh months of Winter, we must never forget, God willing, Spring always returns and with it brings new life."

Nobody spoke as my father folded the paper again and passed it to my mother, who clasped it to her heart. Meanwhile, Ellie shifted closer to me, and I felt her hand slide into mine as we watched the sun dip slowly below the horizon, casting a golden hue over the rolling fields. After a few moments, my sister looked at me as if she was studying some great mystery.

"You've changed, Athena May. You're fancy now, very different from when we went to that first church dance," she paused and sighed, "I bet you don't even remember."
Despite myself, I chuckled and shook my head,

"Oh, I remember it all," I answered firmly, "from taking our shoes off as soon as we left the house to dancing with Samuel Merriweather. That boy trampled every single toe on both of my feet!"
Ellie's eyes beamed with absolute joy at the realisation that for all my 'fancy' ways, underneath it all, I was the same person.

"The boy who looked like a spoon!" she laughed.
"A spoon with the feet of an elephant," I answered, grimacing at the memory.
She laughed again, and together, we began to reminisce about that evening that seemed a long time ago but was actually no more than a few years.
We had both been so excited we drove our parents almost mad with our constant chatter while our hearts fluttered with anticipation. Looking back, I think they were relieved

when we finally left the house, although both of them took us aside and talked solemnly about remembering we were ladies. Our mother had made us both a special dress, and for once, thanks to our grandmother, we were not dressed the same. Ellie's dress was the colour of cornflowers, fitted but spread out into a wide skirt from the waist. As she twirled around our bedroom, her smile was as broad as I had ever seen. My dress was a deep pink, patterned with tiny white flowers that, when I moved, resembled a mass of dancing snowflakes. My father had bought us both a pair of patent shoes, which gleamed like black mirrors reflecting the light and were the finest-looking footwear we had ever owned. Even though we pleaded with our mother, much to our dismay, we were not allowed make-up, so we both bit our lips furiously in a misguided effort to achieve a lipstick effect. We tweaked our cheeks to give them the appearance of being dusted with blush and dampened our eyelashes so they would look curled.

After repeating assurances of good behaviour, at last, we were allowed to leave the house and almost as soon as we knew our watchful parents couldn't see us, both of us took off our shoes. As smart as they looked, they pinched so much it was pure torture to wear them.

"We'll put them back on when we get there," I suggested, to which Ellie readily agreed, quickly adding, "We'll be dancing, so we probably won't notice."

So, we strolled along the dirt road, humming loudly, while our bare feet rhythmically touched the earth as we practised our dance steps, surrounded by the heavy perfume of honeysuckle. Above us, the cobalt evening sky was adorned with a rich tapestry of twinkling stars, gently shimmering as if preparing themselves to join in our evening. When we reached the whitewashed chapel, its doors were wide open like welcoming arms. The sound of joyful laughter and excited conversations spilt into the night, accompanied by the melodious sway of music that rode on the air. Pausing only to put on our shoes, we caught glimpses of colourful dresses twirling in perfect time to the steady drumbeat.

Soon, we found ourselves amidst a sea of glowing faces; as the rhythm quickened, there was no way to resist the beckoning dance floor, so we hesitantly stepped forward, our hearts beating so fast like captured butterflies. Within moments, we were approached by young men in starched shirts fastened with brightly coloured ties. With each step, we shed our inhibitions and embraced the freedom that the dance offered, both finding ourselves swept up by strong but respectful arms that led us around the floor. More than once, I glanced over a broad shoulder and saw my sister. I was sure there had never been anyone more beautiful. Her large eyes shone with glittering wonder at her partner, that dazzling smile and how her slim frame melted seamlessly into her partner as they danced. In comparison, I had almost none of her effortless charm or her flowing movement, but that night, it didn't bother me at all. For me, it was enough when I felt the weight of the world lift from my shoulders as all the worries that usually dominated our days dissolved into the night to be replaced by pure and unadulterated joy.

Ellie and I spun and sashayed, our laughter rising over the music like a joyous choir. Every so often, we would meet by the refreshments table and, while sipping cool lemonade, share our experiences on the dance floor. Giggling at some of our partners' stilted, uncomfortable steps while sighing with undiluted pleasure at those boys who effortlessly carried us as though we were gliding over ice.

Too soon for our young hearts, the evening came to a close, and it was time for us all to go home. After saying goodnight, hand in hand, we made our way back. The night air was cool and damp, silhouetted trees loomed on either side of us, while overhead, their leaves barely rippled in the

dark stillness. But neither of us was fearful, as we were still
dancing, waltzing along the path, illuminated only by the
pale blue light of a friendly moon. Only when a large owl
suddenly appeared, flying silently straight towards us, we
were reminded of the late hour.

When we reached the house, unsurprisingly, our parents
were still awake. Our mother carefully studied us both, like
a keen detective trying to find some clue that proved we
had misbehaved. Luckily, our father insisted we go straight
to bed, so we scampered up to our room without needing to
hear his instructions twice. After neatly folding our clothes,
we dived under the covers, but neither of us could sleep.
For almost an hour, we talked, both speculating on which
boy we might marry one day. I was decidedly unconvinced
by any of them, but Ellie flipped between them all, some
being 'perfect' for no other reason than their smile! The
conversation was brought to a swift halt when our father
called out that he hoped we were asleep, and we obediently
settled down.

When the story was told, I noticed Ellie quickly wipe away
a stray tear from her cheek,

"Why are you crying?" I asked she turned to look at me,
her large eyes filled with such sadness,

"We will never be like that again," she said quietly, "now that you've gone."

I slipped my arm around her and pulled Ellie close, "Yes, we will. You'll come and visit me in the city," I replied firmly, quickly adding that wherever we were, nothing could ever change us being sisters.

"Do you promise?" she asked, "Will I really be able to come?"

When I nodded, she sniffed loudly and wiped her face with her hand before looking at me, her eyes sparkling again. "And we can dance with men who know how to dance, no elephants!"

"No elephants," I laughed.

We hugged tightly and gazed out at the horizon as the last few embers of rich red sunlight glowed like celestial firelight on the tips of the distant hills. At that moment, with only the sound of the night birds calling to each other, I briefly felt my grandmother's presence, reminding me never to forget, and in my heart, I knew I never would.

Feeling profoundly moved, I closed the book and put it back on the cushion next to the rainbow ball. Reading the journal had brought to the surface my own memories of family, especially my grandmother. She had been a small woman but incredibly physically and mentally strong. Even way into her 80s, she could be found at the top of her rickety step ladder and taking down her net curtains so she could wash them by hand. Almost as soon as this image appeared in my mind, I felt a distinct pang of embarrassment as I could guess how she might look at me now. At one time, I probably carried her hope for the future, to be as resilient and eminently capable of coping with everything as she had been. But what had she got instead? A granddaughter for whom life was, at best, something to be endured. Although I had never heard her be unnecessarily critical of anyone within her family, it felt inevitable that were she still alive, it would be impossible to be proud of me. I buried my face in my hands, hardly able to bear the intense feeling of her imagined disappointment. I remained hidden until I felt a familiar presence in the room. Looking up, Athena May was sitting in the armchair, a frown clouding her face.

"What's wrong, child? Why has reading my journal caused you to feel so much pain?"

I shook my head and explained, as best I could, my feelings of failing not only myself but my family. Athena May sighed heavily but, for a few moments, said nothing, but I could see from her expression that silence was necessary to collect her thoughts. When she was ready, she asked me to settle back on the couch and listen carefully without interruption. Having garnered my agreement, she placed her handbag on the floor by her feet, rested her clasped hands on her lap and began to speak.

"Failure can be like a persistent, malevolent spirit haunting even the most righteous people. Or it appears like a ravenous beast, noisily consuming a mind while casting shadows over our brightest hopes and dreams. But, perhaps worst of all, in those near silent moments, when it relentlessly whispers, its sly, venomous voice constantly reminding us of all our imagined shortcomings."

She paused and looked at me, and when seeing some sign that her words were being understood, she continued.

"But what if, my dear Jenna, this feeling of failure is only an illusion, a mirage in the vast desert of life? I know you've been reading about my grandmother. She taught my sister and me, and probably many other people too, that failure does not define anyone, but rather, it can propel us towards even greater heights. It is in these moments, as I think I've mentioned before when everything seems against us that our real strength emerges. Does that make sense to you?"

"So, you're saying failure can be a good thing?" I asked incredulously, "Because if that's true, I should be a world leader by now."

Athena May looked at me sternly, clearly unimpressed with my weak attempt at humour.

"No, child, I am saying something entirely different," she replied firmly, causing me to sink back into the couch, feeling awkward and embarrassed. Seeing my reaction, her frown faded as quickly as it had appeared and was replaced with her familiar warm smile.

"Don't let any failure, real or imagined, stop you from being able to move forward. Embrace every lesson learned and hold onto everything you've gained. For it is in this journey that you will not only overcome, but you will also triumph."

I noticed she had shifted forward towards me as if hoping closer proximity might serve to emphasise her point.

"You can do this, Jenna. I know, right now, you are weighed down with so much doubt, so much grief, it feels impossible to even move. But believe me, I can see it in you, and whatever you might think, your grandmother would see it too."

Her last comment startled me from any self-reflection. How could she possibly know what I'd been thinking? When I asked, I half-expected her to reply with some enigmatic turn of phrase. Still, instead, she simply explained that the journal was open on the page where she'd written about her grandmother, so logically, it would trigger a similar memory for me. Positive, the book was closed. I glanced down and saw it was as she had said. Still feeling vaguely bemused, I shut the journal, and as I did so, my eyes fell on the rainbow ball.

"A young girl came here; she said her name was Miss Elizabeth."

For a moment, I noticed a slight furrow appear on her brow,

Athena May smiled and nodded towards the ball,

"Ah, that precious girl," she said tenderly, "some things never change. She is one of those people that should always be held close, otherwise, they get misplaced or, worse still, be lost to us."

Her tone had a distinct weight of sadness, as if she was recalling something painful, so rather than pry, I opted to ask an innocuous question.

"Should I give it to you, or do you think she'll be back? She wanted to see you," I continued.

"No, you keep it for now," she replied firmly, "hopefully our paths will cross in time."

Before I could say any more, she rose from the chair,

"Do you have to go so soon?" I asked, "There's still some soup left and bread."

Athena May smiled and shook her head,

"Well, you should have some, child; I can tell by your eyes you've been reading for way too long."

She waited until I was in the kitchen, turning on the oven to reheat the soup.

"I'll be back soon, Jenna; trust in that."

From out of nowhere, I heard myself call out to her,

"Are you really here?"

Athena May stopped and looked at me, clearly somewhat surprised by my sudden outburst.

"I have to know," I continued, my voice quivering in that place between tears and confusion, "the way you are here and then you're just gone," I stammered, looking down at the floor before facing her again, "is any of this real or has my mind finally gone completely? Is it all some kind of hallucination? A kind of madness?"

Her eyes filled with such pain as if I could not have said anything more hurtful to her; she shook her head slightly and sighed heavily. "There is no madness in you, child. I am here for you, and I promise, even though I have to leave, I will always come back."

Her words were so laden with genuine sincerity that whatever lingering doubts my mind tried to put forward were quickly swept aside.

"Now, you make sure you eat something," she continued, "I can't have anything happening to you."

As had happened before, she had already gone when I looked back to reply. More than at any other time since I had been in the house, I felt painfully alone, so it was almost out of spite that I continued to prepare the soup. When it was ready, I sat down at the table and began to eat. After only the first spoonful, my body relaxed and allowed the self-enforced tension to dissipate.

"Whatever is in this, it works," I admitted aloud before breaking off another uneven chunk of bread and eating with unexpected pleasure.

I had only just finished clearing everything away when suddenly, a burst of noise came from the hallway; something was repeatedly hammering at the front door. My heart leapt into my mouth when I heard a gruff voice calling out, filled with impatience.

"Police! Is there anyone there?"

I cowered behind the kitchen door, jumping every time the machine gun-like pounding of a heavy hand rattled the rusted hinges of the door. I could barely breathe as the fear of being discovered caused my whole body to tremble uncontrollably. My mind frantically tried to form some kind of logical explanation for why I was there but could only flit like a panicked bird, jumping from one idea to the next, desperately hoping to find the way out. Finally, the incessant banging stopped, and I heard two distinct voices.

"This is a waste of time. I'm hungry. Let's go and get something to eat," one insisted.

"Shouldn't we go round the back? Check nobody's broken into the place?" asked the other, only to be greeted with a groan from their colleague.

"No way, I'm not climbing through a mountain of garbage for no reason. Any idiot can see this place is empty."

I heard a set of heavy footsteps walking away from the door but remained motionless, as I knew two people were outside.

"Come on, Mike," urged the first voice impatiently.

"Yes, go on, Mike," I whispered hoarsely.

At last, I heard his boots thud down the steps, and when I was confident, they had left, it was like the tension had been holding my body upright, and as soon as it dissipated, I had to cling onto the wall to stop from collapsing onto the floor. I took several deep breaths, which seemed to help my anxious mind focus. There was no question; I had to leave the house. The raw fear of them coming back was overwhelming; there would be no peace now. After pulling on my coat and shoes, I scanned the room, my eyes finally landing on the notebook. I hesitated, not knowing whether or not I should take it with me. But the growing panic forced a decision, so I pushed the book into an inside pocket along with the rainbow ball. Hurrying toward the back door, I wished there was time to leave Athena May a note to explain, but instead, all I could do was hope she would understand. I peered through the small, frosted glass panel that was inset into the door frame and was relieved to see it was dark outside. It occurred to me I had no idea how much time had passed since I had come into the house. Unable to make any accurate calculation, I settled on probably about three or four days, which, if I had carried out my original intention, I would never have experienced. "Come on, Jenna, there's no time to stop and think now," I said firmly.

I pressed my ear to the glass; aside from the sound of light rain, it seemed like there was nobody around. After one glance back, I eased the latch and pushed the door open. I felt the cold, damp night on my face and took a deep breath. After the stale mustiness of the house, my lungs seemed to sigh with relief at this welcome intake of clean air. After checking the notebook would remain untouched by the weather, I half ran down the rubbish-strewn alleyway, briefly acknowledged by a couple of rats who were feasting on the remains of a discarded burger. Once back on the street, I walked as quickly and with as much purpose as possible, needing to create distance between myself and the house. As I had no other choice, there was only one place to go, so with great reluctance, I headed home. Trying to ignore the irony that the place that had been my prison was now the only refuge, I hurried along the largely deserted streets. The loyal moon tried to shine and guide my way- yet cruel, dark clouds smothered the silvered light. Every few moments, my path glimmered into view, only for darkness to return seconds later. An unnerving, ancient battle between inescapable gloom and the ever-hopeful light raged in the skies above- leaving me confined to the ground to try and survive on spectral flashes of illumination. I was almost there when St. Anthony's bell rang out over the incessant hum of the traffic. For some reason, I found myself counting the chimes.

"Twelve," I said quietly, stopping outside the 24-hour store to make use of the harsh light as I scrambled through my pockets to find my keys. As I searched, a man unceremoniously dumped a stack of newspapers next to me on the street and went back inside the shop. I idly looked down. There was a banner headline about some politician, but it wasn't what caught my attention. My eyes were drawn to the date, July 4th. That was the day I had left home, so rather than having spent almost a week away, it had barely been 24 hours. I shook my head, utterly unconvinced by my own reckoning and, having found the keys, took the last few steps home. Everything was just as I'd left it, the curtains drawn, everything tidily arranged aside from my phone that had been left discarded on the coffee table. I switched it on while trudging upstairs and into my bedroom. The screen illuminated with a dozen or more notifications, some announcing unanswered calls from unknown numbers. Still, the majority were my therapist, reminding me of appointments we both knew I probably wouldn't attend. I couldn't say for sure which one of us had become more frustrated with those hours spent talking about the same things and making no discernible progress. But just by the number of missed calls, it was obvious she wasn't inclined to give up just yet. Having resolved to at least listen to her voicemails in the morning, I carefully put the notebook on my bedside table. I quickly undressed, wearily slipped under the covers, and picked up the phone to switch it off, but I gasped when I saw the date:

July 5th. It was irrefutable confirmation of how long I had been away. Now wholly bewildered, I looked again, but there was no mistake.

"So, all of that happened in a day?" I exclaimed, utterly unable to make even the slightest sense of what was undeniably the truth. I slumped back onto the pillow and stared blankly up at the ceiling, my mind devoid of any reasonable explanation. It would have been easy to convince myself the whole thing had been nothing more than a dream, that I'd never actually left the house at all. But the presence of the notebook defied the acceptance of that conclusion. I flipped over and tightly closed my eyes, deciding I needed to sleep, hoping that maybe in the morning, my mind would be clearer.

CHAPTER FIVE

When I awoke, I felt momentarily disoriented, as I half-expected to find myself on the old couch and to be back in a proper bed with clean sheets and deep pillows felt almost wrong. So, I lay there, watching the glowing fingers of sunlight steadily steal the last few shadows of night. I could hear the noise of the world waking up outside, the distant, low, rumbling roar of a train thundering over a bridge and even the distinct chatter of people passing under the window. To them, this day was probably like any other, whereas, for me, it was one I had planned never to see. I glanced over at the bedside table; alongside the usual collection of medications, there was Athena May's notebook. Realising the time, I was well aware I should be in the bathroom, taking those pills that promised to help me with my thoughts and yet had done nothing other than leave my mind in a near-constant fog. So, I quickly decided against them and started rearranging my pillows with the plan of rereading the book. I was aware there were still unanswered questions about how long I'd been in the old house, but what did it matter? Perhaps I'd been mistaken in the first place about which night I'd gone out in the rain. The medications were so strong, and I couldn't remember eating that day; maybe they'd just hit me harder, leaving me confused. It wouldn't have been the first time their effect has caused problems. I'd lost days before. Days spent staring at a blank wall without even the slightest grasp on the passage of time. Settling back into the stacked pillows, I carefully put the notebook on my knees, feeling relieved I had at least had the sense not to leave it behind.

The day I stepped into my first home was a day I will never forget. After almost two years of saving every available penny, I finally had enough for the down payment. At first, I procrastinated about making such an investment, but after paying rent for so long, in the end, it just made sense to use my money for my future security. Since arriving in the city, I had been very blessed to not only find my first apartment but also for it to be owned by such a fair landlord, Mr Fiore. Thirty years ago, he had arrived with his then-young pregnant wife with plans for opening a restaurant, and they had achieved their dream and so much more, most importantly in growing their family with four more children. He explained that it was for them. They had expanded into owning property, two small apartment blocks filled with every possible kind of person who he felt needed a place to stay. When I asked him if he had hopes to pass on the restaurant to his children, he chuckled.

"Out of the five, only my daughter, Serafina, shows any real interest in cooking. The others are all aiming for what they tell me are more fulfilling careers," he paused and looked at me solemnly, "I don't argue, but what can be better than feeding your family, am I right?"

He smiled broadly when I heartily agreed and told him a little about how hard my parents had worked and how much I appreciated everything they'd done for me.

"That's because you're smart, Miss Bower," he said, tapping the side of his temple with his finger, "I knew it the first time I met you."

So, it was with a degree of sadness when I told him about my new home, as since I'd been in the city, knowing he was there had been a great comfort. He told me that although sorry to see me go, he understood the need to put down my roots and be in charge of my own destiny. After settling the remainder of the rent, he took my hand and made me promise if I ever needed anything, all I had to do was get in touch. I knew he meant every word as, despite his apparent wealth, whenever anything went wrong in my apartment, it had only ever taken the briefest phone call.

He would appear, dressed in old overalls with his battered old toolbox and endless practical knowledge. The wide range of his expertise never failed to impress me, but when I said anything, he would just shrug and say,

"Why pay someone to do something you can do yourself? Makes no sense to me."

Over the ensuing months, he kindly took the time to show me whenever something needed to be done. So, by the time I was ready to move out, thanks entirely to his patience, I had a very basic knowledge of many household repairs, which would undoubtedly be helpful in my new home.

Ah, that first home; just thinking about it brings a smile to my face. It was small and very cosy, but whoever designed it had made excellent use of every inch of floor space, as it never felt cramped. Outside was a small garden at the front with an even smaller backyard. It was these features, more than any other, that had made me fall in love with the place. Even though when I first saw it, there was nothing much there other than a few straggly blades of rough grass poking through the bare earth. But in my mind, I could see them as patches of pure heaven, filled with blooming flowers and maybe even a small tree to offer some shade in the Summer.

On that first day, as I walked through the front door, I was filled with an overwhelming sense of pride. It was over a week before I stopped looking at my mortgage agreement with my name as a householder written in bold. I remember the way the sunlight streamed in through the windows, casting a warm glow over the hardwood floors. I imagined myself cooking in the kitchen, perhaps one of my grandmother's recipes, entertaining friends in the living room, and relaxing in the backyard on warm summer evenings. As I walked from room to room, taking in every detail, I felt a sense of belonging that I had only previously experienced in my parent's house. But this was my home, my sanctuary, a place where I could build a life and make memories that would last a lifetime.

In the weeks that followed, I poured my heart and soul into making the house my own. Hanging pictures I bought from the market on the walls, planting flowers in the garden, and arranging furniture to create the perfect space. And at the end of the day, I always sat on my front porch in an old cane chair I found in a thrift shop and watched the sunset over the city skyline.

Through those first months, I often thought of my parents; there was always a slight sadness when I did.

Although, in some eyes, I was very fortunate to have a home of my own, they had something so much more that amount of money could buy, a loving partner. I would never be foolish enough to claim they were always blissfully happy. More than once, my mother would storm out of the house, slamming the door with such force that even the china plates on the dresser would shake with fear. Equally, my father would leave but more quietly, always solemnly announcing he needed to take a walk. I used to wonder if when he was far out of earshot, he did his screaming and shouting out there to release his frustration. But if he did, I never witnessed it and neither did anyone else.

So my sadness came from when I had to acknowledge that although it was wonderful to have my own home, I didn't have a special person who could be a part of it all with me. Not that I hadn't had the opportunity, oh no, love had come and gone in my life as the rolling ocean tides ebb and flow on the beach. Sometimes, leaving precious memories in the soft sand like delicately curved seashells to be treasured. Whereas there were other times when the beach had nothing more than the shattered remnants of my heart that had to endure the pain of waiting to be washed away forever.

I shifted position and glanced over at the one photograph I had on display; it was in a decorated silver frame that my late mother had given me years ago. I pretended to myself it was for this reason that the picture had kept its place on my bookshelf, but in my heart, I was well aware that it was a lie. The truth was, I couldn't bear to take it down as it reminded me of a time when life was a place I inhabited with genuine happiness. It showed me with David we were smiling, our faces so close there was barely a hair's breadth between us. His bleach-blonde hair was blown by the wind, creating a kind of glowing halo around his tanned face. His sparkling eyes looked boldly out from the picture as if looking for his next adventure without a trace of trepidation, and there I was, filled with the self-confidence that he had given me. From the moment we met, it was like he had a light inside him that he shared with me, and I eagerly danced within it. He had such a determination to experience everything regardless of his safety, often recklessly taking on challenges that, with hindsight, even he acknowledged were a step too far. And I was his willing partner, happy to fuel his relentless drive to take yet another chance even though I was often secretly terrified. But it was worth every discomfort just to listen to him talk, to feel his touch, to have moments when he literally glowed

with pride when I achieved something with him. I had
spent so long feeling invisible that it was overwhelming
when I realised he not only saw me but loved me. So it
went on, the two of us doing everything together until that
last time, the hike up into the mountains to witness a world-
famous comet blaze fiercely across the night sky. An event
that only happened once in every fifty years. It had been the
subject of folklore for generations, recorded by those
ancient people as a sign, even a message from a divine
being. As soon as David mentioned the story to me,
brimming with his childlike wonder, I knew we would be
going.

As the raw pain of the memory started to take hold, without
really thinking, I reached for the previously dismissed
medication and slammed down three pills in rapid
succession, even though I knew they could do little to have
any discernible impact.

"Don't do this to yourself," I muttered and forced myself to
look away from the picture, desperately trying to immerse
myself back into the notebook. Reasoning that whatever
Athena May might have written about couldn't be as
crippling as the guilt and pure agony I felt when I recalled
that shockingly awful day. But there was no escape; I could
see myself in the hotel room. I had been sick, and so when

the time came to leave, I'd insisted David go without me. At first, he resisted, saying he should miss the trip and stay and look after me. But I knew how much he wanted to go, so I reminded him how rare this moment would be, knowing it would make it an even more irresistible prospect. As I reassured him I would be fine, he looked out the window at the waiting mountain and smiled. After promising to tell me everything, he'd gone, bouncing out of the door, bubbling with enthusiasm. I would never see him again. Never to rest my head on his chest at night as he planned our next adventure or hear that infectious laugh that filled every room in our home with pure, unadulterated joy. In the space of a day, that precious light had gone, and I was plunged back into darkness. The official report stated that the group had been caught out by the onset of unexpected bad weather and reduced visibility. As the light deteriorated, David had probably become separated from the others in the dense mist, lost his footing and simply missed the edge of a steep-sided, deep ravine, falling to his death. The conclusion drawn by the investigation described it as a tragic accident, and there was no one to blame. But I knew the truth, it was because of me. If I had been with him, it would never have happened. We would have worked our way back together. I was certain that if we had never met at all, he would still be alive. The fact he was gone was my fault, and everything that had happened since was only what I deserved, and I knew it. I stared at the pages, but the words swam in front of my eyes, blurred by both my regret-filled tears and the dulling effect of the pills. Accepting it was impossible to focus, I put the book back and pulled the bed covers over my head. I always hoped David would come to me in my dreams, but it never happened. He was lost, and I'd never find him again, not even in sleep.

Hours later, when I awoke, still groggy from the drugs, I sensed there was someone in the room with me. I peered through the darkness and saw a familiar figure sitting in the chair by the window, the edge of their face highlighted by the soft glow from outside.

"Hello, child; I was so worried to discover you had left my house. I needed to check that you were alright; it appeared you had left in something of a hurry."

"The police banged on the door," I stammered as my mind struggled to catch up with the fact of her presence, "I was scared they would come back," I paused and felt compelled to ask how she had managed to get into my room.

"The front door wasn't locked, and I felt we knew each other well enough that I would be as welcome here as you were in my home," she replied calmly before leaning forward slightly, "You've been crying, child, do you want to talk about it?"

As always, just being in the same room as Athena May brought the most intense feeling of peace. Even though there was no physical contact between us, somehow, a genuine warmth wrapped around me, like a comforting, unseen embrace. Despite my usual reluctance whenever David was mentioned, I found myself telling her everything, and she listened intently, her only movement being an occasional slight nod of the head. By the time I was finished, my whole body felt drained, and my face was streaked by the passage of the countless tears that had flowed freely between almost every word I had spoken. Feeling as if there was nothing left to say, I slumped back on the bank of pillows, wiping my eyes on the corner of the bed cover. For several moments, the room was silent until, at last, Athena May told me to turn to the back pages of her journal.

"Although, as you've seen, nearly all the words are my own, I also kept things that were said by others out of fear that, over time, I might forget."

Dutifully, I did as she asked and found a folded sheet of lavender notepaper between the book's pages.

"When my beloved father died, after his funeral at my mother's insistence, I returned to my home in the city. Like everyone who knew and loved him, I was utterly bereft; it felt as if life would never be the same. When I unpacked my suitcase, I found those words from my grandmother. In the depths of her grief, my mother shared them with me to bring comfort, and I would like you to read them aloud to us both."

Although I felt slightly uncomfortable reading something so personal, I could see in Athena May's expression it was what she wanted.

My precious daughter,

In the depth of sorrow, where regretful shadows linger, and bitter tears flow, lies the agony of our loss. It roars within us, thoughtlessly shattering the fragile pieces of our hearts, leaving behind an ache that seems without end.

In those times, never forget, even when life feels at its darkest, there is always hope, for hidden deep within that pain lies the seed of healing. But to find that peace amidst the wreckage, we must be prepared to face ourselves and understand what we need to learn.

Before it's possible to take even that first step, we must find the courage to acknowledge our grief, for it is only then we

will eventually find the strength to heal. So, let the tears
fall, relive the memories, both good and bad, as it's the
very fragility of life that makes every moment so precious.
Finally, you must accept although we may never be entirely
free from our sadness, it need not define us. Never doubt
that love transcends the boundaries of time and space and
that the ones we have lost will continue to speak to us as
echoes in the wind if we choose to listen.
Yours always in love,
Mama

"That's really beautiful," I said quietly while slipping the
paper back inside the book, "Your grandmother was an
extraordinary woman."

"Indeed she was," Athena May replied, "by the time that
was written, she had suffered the pain of loss many times. I
believe it was from her own suffering that her deep
understanding was born."

She paused and looked at me with such an intense focus it
was almost unnerving until she spoke again.

"I know you're grieving, child, and it's not for me to say
which way is right for you, but if you will allow me, I
would like to build on the foundation of my grandmother's
words."

Believing she could help me, I readily agreed, and she rested back in the chair.

"Nobody has ever truly gone, even after they depart from this earth, their soul or, to put it another way, their essence, remains with us. So when we say goodbye, it is not an end but a transformation. Their light continues to shine, and their love, like an eternal flame, burns brightly within us. When the shadowed veil between the seen and unseen grows thin in those quiet moments, we will feel them. Like David, they are there, reminding us that, as my grandmother wrote, love transcends the boundaries of time and space."

When she said his name, my breath suddenly caught in my throat, and it felt like I'd received a sharp blow to my chest. "You're wrong!" I blurted, "All those fine words and clever phrases mean nothing to me. They can't hide the truth, the truth that David isn't here because of me. It's my fault he died."

For the first time since we'd met, I felt nothing but anger when I looked at Athena May. I leapt out of bed and yelled that she knew nothing about him or me, so her opinion was worthless.As I continued to rant, her calm demeanour did nothing but enrage me further until, at last, with my temper at boiling point,

"The people you've lost were old; they were at the end of their lives, but David was different. What do you know about losing someone who was at the beginning?" I screeched, glaring at her with wild eyes, my chest heaving with frantic, shallow breaths.

I saw her shoulders sink as she clasped her hands tightly together on her lap and stared down at the floor.

"Ellie passed when her childhood was still a fresh memory," she replied, her trembling voice barely more than a low whisper. She looked up at me,

"So yes, child, I do know. I know what it feels like to carry the burden of responsibility, to relive moments and pray you could go back and effect a different outcome. I understand all too well how impossible it can be to feel there will ever be a time when you can truly accept that not everything is within your control. To trust there is a purpose, a reason for the most unexplainable, the most painful moments."

Her words hung in the air between us; suddenly, my anger evaporated and was instantly replaced with acute embarrassment at my inexcusable outburst.

"I'm so sorry," I replied, "for your loss and for everything I said."

Her large eyes glistened with the profound sorrow I had caused by forcing such a painful memory to the surface. "You didn't know, but thank you for your apology and your condolences," she replied softly before changing to a slightly more assertive yet kindly tone.

"Now maybe you should go, wash your face, and then consider going outside, child, even if it's just for a short walk in the park; escaping into nature can be very healing." Despite being slightly taken aback by this change, I obediently followed her instructions. Then I returned to the bedroom, ready to talk more. But Athena May had gone. I sank onto the bed; perhaps she had been hurt more by my words than it had appeared, so all I could do now was trust she would return. I glanced at my bedside table and was relieved to see the notebook was still there. As long as it was with me, perhaps my connection to her would remain; it was the one light in my life, and I had to believe it wasn't gone forever. Selfish as it sounded, I knew to be alone in the dark again would be more than I could bear. Not wanting to dwell too much on what might happen in the future, I decided to follow Athena May's advice about going out; perhaps it would help, although it seemed unlikely.

CHAPTER SIX

As the sun's warm embrace gently touched my skin, I
ventured out into the park, hoping for the healing Athena
May had promised. It felt like an eternity since I last
walked along these paths with David. Yet even though he
was not physically with me now, curiously, there were
moments when I was sure I could feel his presence.
Whether it was real or simply wishful thinking, I found
comfort in the sensation, and it helped me to keep going.
My steps were hesitant at first, as if my muscles had
forgotten the rhythm of movement. But with each stride,
energy slowly returned and began to course through my
veins. As I walked amidst the lush greenery, it felt as if
everything around me was breathing life into my weary
bones. The scent of freshly bloomed flowers mingled with
the earthy fragrance of the soil, welcoming me back into
the world. Birds fluttered above, their melodies weaving
delicate symphonies in the air while the gentle breeze
carried whispered words that I convinced myself were only
meant for me.

I watched as families played on the grass, their laughter
echoing through the park. Children ran with unfettered joy,
oblivious to the ever-watchful eyes of their parents. As I

walked between the ancient oaks, I felt like their branches were reaching towards me, like protective arms. The sunlight filtered through their leaves, casting dappled patterns on the ground as if nature herself was painting a masterpiece. At that moment, I could almost believe perhaps the world had not forgotten me but instead had been patiently waiting for my return. I found a wooden bench; it had been created from a fallen tree and hand-carved with evident care to make it comfortable and a piece of art. I settled down on the polished bark and gazed at the serene lake, its surface shimmering in the golden rays of the sun. I watched as water birds gracefully glided, their sleek feathers of grey, blue and white barely breaking the surface. As they swam, their reflections mirrored in the stillness of the lake, a perfect harmony of reality and illusion. Some birds moved in graceful formations; their actions synchronised like a choreographed ballet. In contrast, others dipped their beaks into the water, emerging with glittering droplets that sparkled like diamonds under the sun.

I closed my eyes, allowing the sounds of nature to envelop me. The gentle lapping of the water against the shore, the rustle of leaves in the wind, and the distant chirping of birds all helped to soothe my troubled mind. Suddenly, for no more than a second, I felt something lightly touch my hand. I opened my eyes to see what had disturbed me, but there was nothing. As I closed my eyes again, I heard a whispered voice.

"I'll always love you."

I jumped up from the bench and spun around. Startled by my sudden movement, the birds rose noisily from the lake; their flapping wings caused the now-disturbed water to splash over the stony bank as the thin reeds swayed in protest at the disruption.

"Who said that?" I asked, but there was nobody anywhere near me. Even though I decided it must have been my imagination, all the peace I had felt was gone, leaving me unnerved and suddenly anxious to get home. I half-ran up the path until it felt like there was a safe distance between me and the bench. Taking a deep breath, I stopped to look back and there, at the water's edge, I saw David. I stood frozen, staring at him by the now-tranquil lake, its glassy surface reflecting the afternoon glow of the sun. His presence was undeniable, even though every part of my brain did everything to refute what my eyes were seeing. But he was there, my David, returned to me in a way I never thought possible. The disbelief and awe collided within me, threatening to overwhelm my senses. Time seemed to stand still. I wanted to run to him, but my body felt paralysed; I wanted to call out, but when I opened my mouth, there was no sound. All I could do was watch as he waved to me, his golden hair glowing in the gentle sunlight. He smiled broadly, and I could only stare as he started to turn away. Knowing this would probably be my last opportunity to say anything to him, thankfully, my voice finally returned.

"I'll always love you, David."

As I uttered the last syllable, without warning, silent tears traced the contours of my face. Each droplet held within it a story; a treasured memory carefully written on my heart. For the first time since he'd died, they flowed freely, without restraint, as if determined to finally cleanse the raw wound of my grief that had permeated into every part of my body. I sobbed for all those unfulfilled dreams and all the shared moments that would never be. When I had regained at least some control, I wiped my face on my sleeve and looked back towards the lake, but all I could see were the birds silently gliding down from the surrounding trees to the water. David was gone.

Even though I somehow knew he wouldn't come back, it took all my fragile willpower to walk away. At first, it felt like my feet were encased in lead as I dragged one and then the other. But then I noticed that with every step, it became slightly more manageable, both physically and mentally. I thought back to what Athena May had said about how nobody was ever really gone. Perhaps what had happened was some kind of proof of the truth held within her words. A large part of my mind was still intensely sceptical about whether I'd really seen David. But I couldn't ignore the small voice that simply asked whether it mattered, as the fact it felt real was surely the important thing.

When I was home again, a wave of pure exhaustion hit me, and it was all I could do to make my way upstairs and fall into bed. I had a vague plan to read more of the notebook, but as soon as my head hit the pillow, sleep welcomed me, and I fell willingly into its arms. Despite having felt so weary, my restless mind would only allow me to rest for a couple of hours, and so, to distract my thoughts, I reached for the book.

A new love, like a butterfly, flutters eagerly within the heart. It's a feeling that cannot be contained, like the sun that rises each day in the east. And so it was with me as I walked, hand in hand with Martin. As we strolled between elegant trees, discarded leaves rustled underfoot while the soft breeze touched my cheek with the heady fragrance of wild roses. I felt Martin's hand tighten around mine, and I looked up to see what felt like pure love in his eyes. We walked in silence, content simply to be together.

Eventually, we reached a weathered wooden bridge suspended above the gentle flow of a babbling creek. As Martin led me to the centre, the timbers beneath our feet told tales of the countless travellers and lovers who had crossed before us. Like a glittering silver ribbon, the creek effortlessly wound its way through the rich green tapestry of foliage that had formed on its banks.

I peered into the depths, where life thrived beneath the surface. Tiny fish darted in the sunlight, their scales shimmering with colours, sending a thousand tiny rainbows through the crystal-clear water. Being together in this tranquil place, time seemed to stand still. The rest of the world had somehow melted away, leaving just Martin and me, my head on his shoulder, savouring everything around us. And then, as if on cue, he turned to me, his eyes locked in a moment of perfect stillness. He leaned in, and our lips met in a soft, gentle kiss. It was at that moment I knew I had found my one true love, and it would stay in my memory forever, like a photograph captured in time.

And as we went on our way, the sun setting on the horizon, I felt my heart overflowing with pure, unrestrained joy. For

I was sure that, with Martin by my side, I could weather any storm and conquer every fear. For just as I had read in all those books, from the fairytales of childhood to the intense romances of my youth, it was love that triumphed, love that conquered all, love that made life worth living. And so, with this firm belief entrenched in my mind, I walked with him into the sunset and beyond.

But I was wrong; after only a few short months, everything changed. The sun no longer shone as brightly, and the leaves underfoot had dried and turned to dust. The countryside, once filled with the warm, heady aromas of a romantic Summer, had turned into a harsh Winter of heartache and loss. Now, as I walked, my steps were heavy, and my heart shattered like glass. The bridge over the creek was no longer a magical place teeming with life; now, it stood empty and barren. Even the fish had disappeared, perhaps unable to face me. I leaned over, tears streaming down my cheeks, my heart heavy with pain as I wondered how it had all gone so wrong. Martin, once the light in my life, had left me heartbroken and alone. The promises of love and forever had evaporated like a dawn mist in the morning sun.

It was only after some considerable time I finally straightened up and wiped away my tears, accepting, with *a heavy sigh, that no amount of crying could turn the clock back. Looking forward, I knew even though the days ahead would be difficult, I had to try and be strong enough to face them. As I walked away from the creek, the sun was setting, its warm glow spreading across the sky like a fireside quilt, and at that moment, a thought came to my mind. Perhaps there was some small comfort in the knowledge that I had loved and been loved, which meant there was always the possibility it could happen again.*

As the days turned into weeks and weeks turned into months, the pain of the breakup slowly faded, and I started to focus on rebuilding my life. But then, one day, as I was walking down the street, I saw Martin. My heart skipped a beat as memories flooded back, and I felt a mix of anger and sadness wash over me. Still, I approached him, and after the initial awkwardness, we finally talked. He apologised for what he had done, for lying about so many things, ranging from his past, his job, and, in fact, almost everything he had ever told me. But still attempted to defend himself, saying it was only done in some desperate attempt to impress me. He asked for my forgiveness and made promises to be truthful in the future while repeating, over and over again, that whatever else, he had loved me. Much as I could understand that so much had probably

sprung from his insecurities, the damage had been done,
and I knew I could never trust him again.

Thankfully, the scars healed over time. I met new people,
some making a fleeting impression while others garnered a
permanent place in my affections. I also pursued my
passions and found joy in the simple things in life. The
whole experience with Martin was unquestionably painful
and sometimes felt like an emotional obstacle that I would
never overcome. But of all the lessons it taught me,
believing in the power of hope was the most important. If
that had proved impossible, my life would not have been as
blessed with so many wonderful experiences.

For the first time, I wanted to close the book. I urged my
reluctant hand to put it down, but something made my
hesitant fingers turn the page. I saw a sheet of lined paper
had been carefully glued onto the page of the book. In
Athena May's handwriting, there was a short sentence
saying she had found this piece of writing and had no real
idea of where it had come from. But it was so profoundly
moving she had copied the words to preserve it.

Hope is a bird that soars high above us, taking flight on
wings of possibility and promise. It sings a sweet melody, a
song of resilience and faith, that echoes through the valleys

and hills of our lives. With a heart full of courage, hope inspires us to dream, to reach for the stars, and to believe that anything is possible. It is the light that guides us through the darkest of times.

I read the passage many times, thinking that maybe the repetition would somehow force this message into my mind. Hope was not an emotion that had ever really gained much of a hold on my mind; if it had been there at all, it had the tiniest of voices and so could rarely be heard above the general chaos of my thoughts. After closing the book, I made a firm promise to myself that I would go back to the park in the morning. I knew David wouldn't be there, but I had to admit, as Athena May had suggested, being outside had helped. So it felt logical; I would benefit again.

The following day, I packed the book into my laptop bag, as it felt as if it would offer the best protection and went back to the hollowed bench. The sun was already gently caressing the tops of the trees as if it was delicately gilding the leaves with the softest gold. As I breathed in the scene around me, I closed my eyes so I could completely focus on the lively melodic exchanges between the songbirds nestled in the high branches overhead. Suddenly, I became aware of someone else sitting next to me. As I turned, there was

Miss Elizabeth; she smiled broadly and nodded down towards her feet that couldn't reach the ground.

"I'm so small. This feels like sitting in a giant's chair." Before I could answer, she asked if I had brought her rainbow ball with me. When I shook my head, a slight frown crossed her face.

"Are you sure? Have you checked your coat?" Not wanting to seem dismissive, I started to search through each pocket in turn, even though I was positive they were all empty. However, just as I rummaged into the last one, my fingers touched something and much to my complete surprise, it was the ball.

"There!" she said gleefully, clapping her tiny hands, "I knew you had it. Will you throw it for me? As hard as you can," she pointed over to a small clump of trees, "see if you can reach them."

She slipped off the seat and looked at me expectantly, her eyes sparkling with excitement. After briefly glancing down at my bag, wishing I could just start to read, I stood up and took a couple of steps.

"OK, I'll do my best," I said, pulling my arm back as far as it could go before hurling the ball as hard as possible into the air. Before I had a chance to say any more, the little girl had taken off in the direction of the ball, running so fast, it was as if she were almost flying through the long grass. I saw her disappear into the trees and waited for her to return, but there was no sign after several minutes. For a moment, I thought about going after her but opted to maybe stay at the bench as then she would know where I was and could return when she was ready. I settled back down, pulled my bag onto my lap, and immediately realised it was far lighter than it should have been. I almost ripped it open, but my fear was confirmed: Athena May's notebook was gone. Panic washed over me, consuming my thoughts and leaving a hollow ache in my chest. I had lost it - my most cherished possession. My heart pounded with anguish and disbelief as I frantically looked again and then scoured every inch of the bench. Memories of its worn pages and the familiar scent of ink and paper flooded my mind. Each slightly dog-eared corner held significance, marking a passage that had resonated deeply within me. I retraced my steps along the path, flipping between looking at the ground and then around me, hoping to see someone holding the notebook, but the park was almost deserted. Despite the futility of my search, I kept hoping that by some miracle, I had simply dropped it and, at any moment, would be found again. But the truth hung heavy in the air, mocking my efforts. The book was gone, slipped through my fingers like a fleeting dream.

A wave of emotions surged through me, brought by a tide of grief and regret. How could I have been so stupid, so blind to its absence? The weight of its loss settled upon me, a burden too heavy to bear. I longed to retreat into the solace of its pages, to find comfort and understanding within its words. Having no choice, I reluctantly made my way home, the journey feeling longer than ever before. My bedroom walls seemed to look at me with pure contempt, their emptiness a stark reminder of what I had lost. The silence echoed in my ears, amplifying the ache in my heart. The absence of that book left a void, an emptiness that seeped into every corner of my existence. Tears welled in my eyes as I knew the journal had become far more than just an object; it was a part of me. It had begun to shape my thoughts, whisper truths in the darkest hours, and even ignited a fire within my soul. But now its absence left me feeling untethered, adrift in a sea of uncertainty.

Still clothed, I slipped under the bed covers, repeatedly cursing myself for being so careless. But the more my thoughts whirled and tumbled around my mind, one question rose above all the others as if demanding to be addressed. How had the book fallen out of a closed bag? I sat up and retraced the day's events, but nothing offered any immediate answer. After all, it was only when I threw the ball for Miss Elizabeth that my hands had left the bag. Suddenly, the image of us at the bench appeared with intense clarity came to my mind. When I had stood up, she was behind me and almost as soon as the ball had been thrown, she had run after it, not pausing to say anything to me.

"She took the notebook!" I exclaimed aloud, my despair echoing through the otherwise silent house. I sank back into the pillow, forcing myself to accept there was nothing I could do. Aside from the fact I had no idea where Miss Elizabeth lived or even her last name, there was no way of knowing why she had taken the book. If it was simply some kind of mischievous prank, when she eventually returned to the bench and found me gone, the chances were, she would probably just throw it away. The book was gone forever, taking the last drop of hope for my life to have any kind of future. I had found a special kind of companionship within its pages, but now, through my carelessness, I was alone again. The burden of this realisation pressed upon my chest like an invisible force pinning me down to the bed. I lay there, trapped in the clutches of my own mind, as the days blurred together in a haze of darkness. The demon of my depression had taken hold, its tendrils wrapping around me, slowly suffocating any glimpse of light.

The room around me was shrouded in shadows, the once-familiar objects now distant and unfamiliar. I could hear the muffled sounds of life outside my window, the world moving forward while I remained suspended in this stagnant existence. But I couldn't find the strength to join them, for my energy had been drained, replaced by an overwhelming numbness. Every movement felt like an insurmountable task, each step requiring a herculean effort. I was physically and mentally paralysed as the depression settled on my limbs. My body felt heavy, as if gravity had multiplied its force solely for me. It took all my energy to lift my hand, my fingers trembling under the strain.

Time lost meaning in this cocoon of despair. Hours bled into days and days into weeks as I lay motionless beneath the covers. The world outside my window spun on, oblivious to the war raging within my soul. Yet, I was a prisoner, trapped in this void where darkness reigned supreme. I cried out for Athena May to come, even though, logically, I knew there was no possible way of her being able to hear me. But even if she had, my sleep-deprived mind reasoned there was ample excuse for her to turn away from me. I had broken my promise to care for her work, which could be impossible to forgive even to someone with her level of compassion. Tears cascaded down my cheeks like a waterfall, and the isolation became a self-imposed sentence, a sentence with no end.

My mind became a whirlwind of self-doubt and self-loathing. I questioned my worth and my purpose as a storm of negative thoughts engulfed me. It howled in my ear, an unending haunting chorus of despair, telling me I was unworthy of happiness, of love, of life itself. Cruelly reminding me that it was my fault the book was lost, much as it had been when David died, and that I was destined never to be able to hold onto anything precious because of my own failings.

But deep within this darkness, suddenly, a tiny ember of an idea started to flicker, fragile yet resilient. Crafted with the delicacy of a butterfly's wing, I waited for it to crumble beneath the storm. Yet as I sat, the thought refused to be ignored or swept away- I finally surrendered to its soft, tenacious call. I pulled myself free from the tangled sheets and prepared to return to the abandoned house.

CHAPTER SEVEN

I stood before the old house, its weathered facade glistening under the moonlight. Raindrops dripped from the eaves, their echoes filling the air with a rhythmic melody. The scent of rain lingered in the air, mingling with the earthy aroma of the overgrown garden. After all the despair of the past weeks, I felt all the welcome memories softly tugging at my heart, pulling me deeper into the familiar aura of the building. The house stood in silence, its windows reflecting the night sky like darkened mirrors. I reached out, my fingers grazing the peeling paint that clung to the wooden door. It was a touch that bridged the gap between the past and present.

As I stepped inside, the stillness of the night seemed to permeate every corner. The air was heavy with the weight of all those conversations I had shared with Athena May as if the house held those moments within its walls. I wandered down the hallway, tracing the well-worn grooves etched into the banister. Unlike my previous visit, I glanced into other rooms; a few pieces of abandoned furniture draped in sheets stood like grey ghosts, covered in thick dust.

In the silence, I could almost hear the faint murmurs of my thoughts as I entered the living room, still dominated by the threadbare couch with the ragged blanket neatly folded and draped over one arm.

Outside, the rain stopped, leaving a world shimmering with possibilities for others. I gazed through the tattered curtains, momentarily captivated by the city's twinkling lights, before turning away and settling back onto the sofa. Not having made any specific plan, I wrapped the blanket around my shoulders and pulled a cushion to rest my head. As I did so, I heard a gentle slapping sound on the floor. Looking down, I could hardly believe my eyes; the notebook was lying on the thin gap between the exposed floorboards and the faded carpet. Tearfully overjoyed, I grabbed it and held the book tightly in my arms, silently promising I would never let it become lost again. I looked around and realised Miss Elizabeth was watching me from the doorway, as when we had first met, she was partially hidden behind the frame. At first, I wanted to be angry with her for stealing the book, but seeing the worried frown on her young face, I chose a different path.

"Thank you for giving it back," I said quietly. For a moment, there was silence, but then she tentatively took a couple of steps until I could see all of her. She fidgeted, looking down while twisting her fingers and shifting her weight from one foot to the other.

"I'm sorry," she mumbled, "I shouldn't have taken it, but I was just so mad, I didn't think."

"Were you mad with me?" I asked. She slowly shook her head but didn't say any more.

"Well, I have it back now, so no harm done," I continued, trying to sound comforting, but the child still didn't seem able to look at me. I was about to speak again when she suddenly turned and half-ran along the hallway. I immediately got up from the couch to try and follow her, but by the time I reached the doorway, the hallway was empty. She had obviously slipped out through the front door, which, it was very likely, I hadn't closed. When I checked, it turned out not to be locked. I firmly dropped the latch, remembering the previous unexpected visit from the police. I certainly didn't want them to be able to just walk in on me. Feeling secure, I went back to the couch, pulled the blanket over my knees and held the book in my hand. Turning those pages was like holding the hands of a dear friend I hadn't seen in a long time, and when I found the next entry, I settled down to listen to them talk.

Since owning my home, going against every value I had been taught, I started to prize material possessions, spending time rearranging every room when a new piece of

114

*furniture arrived, or I bought a new piece of art. I would
stand and gaze at every purchase with a level of smug self-
satisfaction, which, now I look back, was distinctly
unpleasant. But at the time, it felt entirely justified; like a
preening peacock, I would almost strut between rooms,
feeling that I was quite the success story. But as tends to
happen in life, there was a completely unexpected incident
which made me stop, reconsider and remember everything
my family had instilled in me since the day I was born.
I don't think I could ever forget the day of the house fire in
my neighbourhood. Far above us all, the sky was the
clearest blue, and the Summer sun was shining. But down
on my street, everything was engulfed in fierce flames. The
thick air was filled with dense, choking smoke and the
sound of crackling embers, like a thousand tiny
firecrackers exploding at the same time. I watched in
horror as the fire hungrily devoured everything in its path,
determined to reduce a once beautiful home to nothing
more than a pile of smouldering ash. The intense heat was
almost suffocating, and the sheer scale was overwhelming.
Brave firefighters rushed into the house, somehow
managing to ignore the weight of their equipment as they
risked their lives to rescue the occupants.*

All I could do was stand at the edge of the chaos, my eyes staring in horror at the billowing inferno. Flames danced in a violent ballet in a frenzy. It seemed as if they were seeking out the memories and dreams of the family, driven by an insatiable hunger to destroy them all. The dire symphony of splitting wood and shattering glass echoed through the neighbourhood, making us all an unwilling audience to the devastation.

Confronted by such carnage, my priorities dramatically shifted like tectonic plates beneath my feet. The superficial lust for material possessions that had dominated my thoughts showed itself as being nonsensical and trivial. The fire served as a merciless reminder to stop, reevaluate and reassess the choices that had, until this moment, begun to shape my days. As the smoke dissipated, carrying floating, blackened ashes into the sky, I vowed to be more mindful of those relationships within my life and pay infinitely less attention to needing more of anything that can be bought. That evening, I sat down and began writing letters to those friends I knew had not received the kind attention from me that they richly deserved. For me, there was one person who would always be at the top of any such list: my friend from home, Cassie. As I paused, trying to decide what to say, I thought about the precious gift of having someone who knows you, truly knows you, and loves you just the same as Cassie had always done. She was far more than just a friend; she was a confidant, a partner in crime, and a source of comfort and support through life's many ups and downs.

I rested back in my chair and thought about when we were children and felt the glow that was carried by such happy memories. We would spend hours talking, sharing our deepest fears and our wildest dreams, and laughing until our bellies ached. We would go on adventures together, exploring the world around us and making memories that would last a lifetime. She had been a constant in my life, a beacon of light in the darkest of times and a rock upon which I could always rely. With her by my side, I had felt invincible, as if nothing could ever stand in our way. Now, with the warmth of this recollection fresh in my mind, I shifted forward and began to write. This is the first draft of the letter I sent, but I wanted to keep it as a lasting reminder of the joy of true friendship.

My dearest Cassie,
I hope you and all those closest to you are well and thriving. I am profoundly sorry for not reaching out to you sooner. There is no excuse, and I sincerely hope you will

find it in your heart to forgive me. There was recently a house fire in my neighbourhood, and it made me reevaluate my priorities, which, sad to say, have been in the wrong order for way too long. I have been thinking back, and with your indulgence, I would like to share some of those thoughts with you.

In the hazy nostalgia of my childhood, I can recall all those enchanting moments spent with you, each one filled with mischief and laughter. Together, we shared a time of innocence, where time knew no boundaries and imagination held no limits.

Do you remember how we would chase the sun in the golden hours of the afternoon, our bare feet dancing on the dusty pathways? How we would always pull off our shoes and wriggle our toes in the long grass? Our mothers would frown and scold us both for looking like wild savages! I remember sitting with you underneath the sprawling oak tree in the far corner of the cornfield; it was our secret hideaway. We would spend hours there, making daisy chains while sharing all our most personal dreams.

Skipping stones across the glistening lake, we revelled in the rhythmic ripples that mirrored our laughter. We chased fireflies, their flickering glow illuminating the night like tiny stars fallen from the heavens.

We always found comfort in one another's presence. Our hearts intertwined like vines, believing they could never untangle and become separated from each other. Through all those years of whispered secrets, we became steadily closer while also being fierce guardians when faced with anything that threatened our precious bond.

But despite all our efforts, Time, that relentless thief finally stole us away from our idyllic haven. The years carried us on separate paths, our lives diverging like rivers flowing toward different seas. But the memories of those cherished moments remain etched in my mind, as impossible to fade as if they had been carved in stone.

Oh, how I long for those days when the world was small, and our hearts were vast with possibility. What I would give to be back under that oak tree and talk with you again! Even as that wild savage, who at times reduced my mother to a rare level of frustrated despair, I was wise enough to know that a best friend is a rare and precious gift that should be cherished and nurtured at every opportunity.

So, my dearest Cassie, I wanted to make sure you knew the spirit of our friendship remains as strong as ever in my heart.

I hope you will understand why it was so important to me to reach out this way, and maybe you'll even feel inclined to reply.

Take very good care of yourself,

Love always,

Athena May

I posted the letter with more anxiety than I'd felt in a long time, and when I knew it must have arrived at her home, I waited with all the nervous anticipation of a child on Christmas Eve. But all my fears proved to be unfounded, as only a matter of days later, she called me, and we talked for hours. It was almost as if the years in between had never happened. We were still those two young girls who saw sleeping giants instead of distant hills and carefully stepped over toadstools, as we were sure they were the homes of magical fairies.

After the house fire, I found myself deeper in thought than usual, often politely turning down invitations and spending time alone. I pored over lengthy academic essays, trying to force myself to be less frivolous and more what I had mistakenly decided was somehow worthy. Although there is no question that reflection can be enormously beneficial, for those friends closest to me, it seemed it had gone on for too long. One Saturday evening, a group arrived at my door, and that evening will always be highlighted in my memory as the time I rediscovered the power of laughter. As while in the depths of my quest to spend more time on worthwhile activities, simply having fun had been markedly absent. We were gathered in my small, cosy living room, surrounded by the warmth of the fire and the sound of the rain tapping against the windows.

As the night wore on, we began to share stories, jokes, and anecdotes, each one funnier than the last. We laughed until our sides hurt, tears streaming down our faces, gasping for breath. As the joyous night wore on, I felt a connection that had been forgotten. It was like we were all part of a secret club, the kind where only those who knew how to relax and have a good time could join. And so, the evening continued into the night until the rain stopped and the fire burned low. Even as we said our goodbyes, I knew the memory would stay with me forever.

While clearing away the glasses, I resolved it was time to create a balance between being alone and maintaining all those relationships which were so vital for making life worth living.

Finally, for those directly affected by the tragedy of the house fire, it will always be a painful memory of all the things that were lost. My sincere wish for them is the same now as it was then, that despite the pain of loss, in time, they can learn to laugh again and always be surrounded by love.

I found the last sentence almost too painful to read, so I closed the book, knowing I needed a break from reading. I rested back on the battered cushion and allowed my eyes to close, even though the lingering fear of being discovered was omnipresent. When I awoke, my heart skipped a beat as there in the armchair sat a figure so familiar yet seemingly had been lost in time. It was Athena May - the one I had believed to be gone forever.

A rush of emotions flooded over me; thoughts swirled like autumn leaves caught in a gust of wind. Time seemed to stand still as I looked steadily at her. I was relieved to see her face hadn't changed; the same lines etched around her eyes spoke of laughter shared, of tears shed, of a life lived. Yet, for all the comforting familiarity, there was a haunting vulnerability in her gaze, as if she couldn't believe this moment was real.

The air crackled with unspoken words, the weight of our brief history filling the space between us. I watched as she looked up, her eyes meeting mine, recognition dawning like a sunrise after the darkest night. A smile, tinged with both joy and sorrow, played at the corners of her mouth.

"Hello, child, I have been so worried about you; for a time, it seemed as if you had become lost, and that deeply saddened me, as I had come to believe we were friends."

"Things have been difficult," I began hesitantly, not knowing whether or not to mention losing the notebook. Athena May nodded but said nothing. It was as if she knew what had happened but wanted me to have the courage to tell her. Feeling like an errant child confessing to a caring mother, I took a deep breath and explained about Miss Elizabeth and throwing the rainbow ball.

"But it wasn't her fault," I said quickly, interrupting myself, "She is only a child. I should have known better. I am so sorry; I should never have even thought about taking the notebook to the park."

The nervousness in my voice was blindingly apparent, and I hoped it showed just how much this whole incident had mattered to me. But throughout, Athena May simply maintained constant eye contact as if she was looking for even the slightest sign of insincerity on my part. When I couldn't think of anything else to say, I sat back and waited for her to either give me a stern reprimand or, worse still, order me out of her home. But when she finally looked away from me, her gaze only travelled far enough to settle on the book.

"I'm curious, child, if my journal was misplaced in the park, how can it be here now?"

"I really don't know," I replied truthfully, "all I can say with any certainty is that Miss Elizabeth returned it when she found me back here."

A slight frown furrowed the old lady's brow,

"Did she explain why she had taken it from you?"

I shook my head as all I could do was repeat what the child had said that she had been mad. On hearing this, Athena May nodded knowingly and rested back in the armchair, offering no further insight into the child's actions. But any possible curiosity I might have felt was quickly surpassed by just being with her again. Someone I had almost started to believe might be nothing more than a mere figment of imagination stirred by a potent cocktail of longing and gratitude within me. But now, in the comfortable silence, the world seemed whole again, as if a missing piece of my existence had been restored.

"Tell me, have you forgiven the child?" Athena May asked.

"I believe so," I replied slowly; this answer pleased her as she smiled broadly.

"I am relieved, Jenna. I read somewhere that to find forgiveness is to embrace the power of compassion and empathy."

Before she continued, Athena May shifted position while putting her handbag down by the side of the chair.

"Of course, forgiving others is not always easy. It can be painful to confront how we have been hurt by those we care about. But I believe that forgiveness is essential to our own healing and growth. When we hold onto anger and resentment, it only hurts us in the end."

"So, how do you forgive people?" I asked in a far more abrupt tone than I had intended. The old lady smiled and pondered for a moment,

"Well, I try to approach them with an open heart and mind while remembering we all have weaknesses. And when I can forgive, I feel a sense of freedom and peace that cannot be found in holding onto grudges and bitterness. It's not about condoning bad behaviour or excusing harmful actions; instead, I believe, it's choosing to extend grace and compassion."

While considering the wisdom of her words, I noticed her lean forward and look at me,

"Now I have a question for you, child: Can you extend similar grace and compassion to forgive yourself?"

Seeing I was taken aback, she continued,

"You have carried the weight for so long, child, don't you think it's time to finally put it down? To show yourself the same compassion and understanding that made it possible for you to forgive Miss Elizabeth with such ease."

"I suppose I could try," I croaked, forcing my response over the large lump in my throat. Satisfied with this answer, she settled back in the armchair.

"You know my grandmother used to recite this passage. I can't be sure if it came from her own mind or from a book she may have read. Either way, it has always resonated with me. In the realm of relentless possibility, where dreams and reality intertwine, trying becomes the anthem of the courageous soul, for in the face of uncertainty, it stands as the unwavering testament to the indomitable spirit of human endeavour."

I did nothing to conceal my amazement at such powerful words but quickly added what felt like a truthful disclaimer. "I don't believe I am a courageous soul."

Athena May shook her head,

"Child, you are here, that alone proves the strength of your spirit."

As I couldn't think of any reasonable response, particularly as she had spoken with such total conviction, I smiled and pulled the blanket until it was over my knees again.

"So, you have learned a great deal about me," Athena May said, nodding toward the notebook, "maybe it's time for me to hear more about you."

Perhaps something in my expression betrayed the fact that I had no desire to revisit my past. But there was also denying she had shared her life experiences. Even though I couldn't ignore my discomfort, I wrapped the blanket a little tighter and decided to talk. Still, after only a few moments, not a single word came out of my mouth.

"I'm not sure where to start," I stammered. Athena May smiled and suggested it might be easier for me if perhaps she asked a few questions, quickly reassuring me that there was no pressure to say anything.

"If you find yourself on a path that will cause you pain, just turn back, and I'll say nothing more."

With this agreement, she asked about my family, on the face of it, a fairly innocuous question, but, for me, it was difficult to answer. But looking at her kind and gentle face encouraged me to speak openly; despite all that therapy, this was probably the first time in my life. I began by talking about growing up, remembering how, in the notebook, the first line was about starting at the beginning. "Well, for most of my childhood, it felt like my parents were wholly focused on their own lives and ambitions. So, when they were in the house, it was as if I was sharing our home with ghosts, as their presence was so fleeting I was never sure if they were there or not. When they did talk to me, it was nothing more than half-hearted murmurs, lost in their obvious disinterest. When they had guests, I'd find myself surrounded by superficial smiles and strained conversations, so I quickly learned to retreat into my imagination."

I paused as my words sounded self-pitying, and I even momentarily doubted whether I was being fair to them. But Athena May quickly reassured me that everyone's recollections can vary, and none more so when retelling a family story.

"It's all about perception," she explained, "People can look at the same thing and see a different side, it all depends on where you're standing."

Feeling slightly better, I continued by focusing on my mother, as I barely knew my father, as they were divorced when I was no more than ten years old. He had left the family home and, as far as I knew, made no genuine attempt to stay in contact throughout my childhood.

"When I was very young, after he had left, it seemed to me that she was a woman who was always preoccupied and remote, but then, as the years passed, I slowly started to realise the painful truth. The dark shadows on her face resulted from countless sleepless nights, while her days were an endless cycle of work and worry, a never-ending battle to keep our fragile world intact."

"It must have been very hard for her," Athena May said quietly, "I can only hope she had some support or perhaps could lean on her faith."

I shook my head, suddenly feeling a long-forgotten but still all-too-familiar feeling of dread in the pit of my stomach, which always happened when the truth about my mother had to be told.

"Looking back as an adult, I think it probably started innocently enough: a glass of wine to unwind after a long day. But as the pressures mounted and the weight of her life grew heavier, that single glass multiplied into a crutch she desperately clung to for some comfort. Alcohol had become a temporary escape from the overwhelming responsibilities, and I could do nothing."

I was aware that my fingers were now gripping the edge of the blanket so tightly that my knuckles were white and almost painful, so I forcibly relaxed my hands. But there was no way of hiding the tremor in my voice as I continued to say more.

"I watched as my mother transformed before my eyes. Her personality, which everyone around her routinely described as vibrant and contagious, was slowly replaced by a hollow, distant echo. Her voice, which had always been filled with confidence, as if there was no doubt that every word she uttered was right, turned into bitterness and regret."

"She was a ship lost at sea, adrift in a storm of her own making," mused Athena May, as if she was talking to herself rather than speaking to me.

"I tried to save her," I answered defensively, "but I was just a child."

The urgency in my voice seemed to startle Athena May out of her thoughts, and she looked at me with such compassion that it was all I could do not cry.

"Child, I understand," she said, her voice barely more than a whisper, "You became an observer in her life, witnessing the slow erosion of her spirit. You held your breath as she stumbled through the door, her steps unsteady, her words slurred. You tiptoed past her room, afraid of stepping on the broken fragments of her shattered dreams that littered the floor."

I sat back, stunned by the accuracy of her words that seemed to come from a place of personal experience. Sensing my surprise, Athena May continued,

"A long time ago, I had someone in my life who struggled similarly, and though I couldn't save her from her demons, I vowed to be a guiding light, a beacon of unwavering love amid her storm," she paused and wiped the corner of her eye with her handkerchief, "but I ultimately failed."

The air between us seemed filled with tangible sadness for a moment, but then Athena May abruptly asked me to tell her more about my life. Somewhat taken aback by this sharp change of subject, I complied and began to talk about school.

"With things as they were at home, I hoped the outside world might offer something better, but it wasn't to be. School seemed full of cliques, groups of girls who gleefully whispered rumours and passed judgment on anyone not like them. At first, I tried, but fitting in felt like an impossible task, especially as I was sure they all knew about my mother. So as the days turned into weeks, weeks into years,

I became more and more lonely until it became a way of life."

Athena May frowned before asking if she might interrupt; I was not quite sure what to expect, so I simply nodded.

"I am not doubting your words, child, please believe that," she began carefully, "but do you think it might be time to question the certainty of your recollections?"

"What do you mean?" I replied more abruptly than I intended.

"Could it be that the weight of everything you have experienced clouds your vision and obscures any moments of compassion and tenderness that may have lived in the hearts of those you encountered along the way?"

I wanted to shoot back with a definitive response, but the words became trapped in my head, lost in a sudden swirl of confusion. Sensing my unease, Athena May continued, "You see, child, in my own life, there have been times when I've had to peel away the layers of cynicism and embrace the possibility that I may have been wrong. I have had to remind myself that kindness exists even in the unlikeliest of places."

Her words hung in the air between us, and I noticed she settled into her chair as if waiting for me to process their meaning before saying anything else.

In the silence, I searched back through my memories while my mind tried to absorb the suggestion that maybe she was right. There was no question many of the students were awful, but was I really their only target? As the question formed, suddenly, it was as if a curtain had lifted on a stage within my thoughts, and a small cast of characters was gazing out at me. Each one wearing the school uniform, many with torn sleeves, some clutching sodden backpacks that dripped from being thrown into a toilet bowl while others were clearly bruised. But it was the most petite girl at the end of this row, her large glasses giving her the look of a nervous owl,

"Isabella Thorne," I said quietly.

Athena May shifted slightly and asked me to tell her more about this particular girl. I didn't know why, but it took me another few moments to fully recall the memory. Still, when I began to talk, it steadily grew in clarity, like a blurred picture being brought slowly into sharp focus.

"I had never spoken to her, but this one afternoon, we were all getting changed after hockey practice. Like always, I was trying to hurry, but one of the girls grabbed the back of my bra and was trying to undo the clasp. They were all laughing, threatening to push me outside.." I paused and swallowed hard as I could almost feel the utter horror that my younger self had experienced.

"You said they were all laughing," Athena May prompted, "even Isabella?"

When the whole scene came into my mind, I gasped, "No," I exclaimed, "she told them to stop. They were all so much bigger than her, yet she pushed herself between them and me. There must have been something about her, as they cursed but backed away," I paused and looked at Athena May, "Why would they do that?"

"Cowards are only brave when they're in company," she replied, "when confronted with someone who chooses to stand tall, regardless of their physical stature, and show true defiance, the weaker will always run. As being faced with such strength of character is far more intimidating than anything they could possibly conceive. But what happened next?"

"They all left until there was only Isabella and me left; she asked me if I was alright and offered to walk with me to our next class," I replied.

"What did you do?" Athena May persisted. I didn't want to answer, especially when my face flushed with embarrassment. Still, despite my discomfort, I admitted to snapping and telling her to just leave me alone.

"I shouldn't have done that," I continued, "she deserved better."

"That's true, but you were young and frightened. Also, it won't help you or Isabella to spend time dwelling on a past error that cannot be rectified. But, here in the present, I hope you can see what I meant, child, that kindness does exist even in the worst places. When you look back again, try using a different lens, one with all the world's colours and not just varying shades of grey."

Athena May acknowledged my nod of understanding and then asked what happened when I had left school.

"Well, when my mother passed, only a day or two after her funeral, my father appeared and suggested the house should be sold. But it seemed she had anticipated the possibility of his intervention, so everything was in the hands of the lawyer. It was all left to me, so when he realised there was nothing for him, my father left, and I haven't seen him again."

"So even in the depths of her utter despair, she was thinking of you," Athena May mused, "you were the one small, flickering light in all that awful darkness."

"I suppose I was," I admitted, feeling strangely unbalanced without understanding the cause, so I quickly continued by explaining that, for the longest time, I lived alone and rarely went out.

"But then, one day, I was at a coffee shop, and I saw David, and it felt as if the whole world shifted, and there was now a glimmer of hope."

After reliving everything else that had been so difficult to talk about, I felt my whole body relax at the mention of his name, and even a slight smile played on my lips.

"He grinned at me and came over; we talked for more than an hour," I said dreamily before remembering Athena May, "I almost missed collecting my coffee; they called my name at least twice before I heard them," she smiled broadly and urged me to finish the story.

"So anyway, we arranged to meet in the park later. It was a warm summer evening; the air was heavy with the scent of flowers, and it seemed the trees were filled with hundreds of birds, all chirping and singing to each other. David walked towards me with so much confidence, his eyes locking with mine in an instant, and suddenly, I felt a rush of emotion, a mix of excitement and nervousness that left me breathless. The longer we were together, the more I became almost spellbound by his intelligence and charm.

He had a way with words that left me hanging on every sentence. There was just something about him that made me feel a bit light-headed as if all the weight I had been carrying for so long was just lifted from me. Does that make sense?"

Athena May smiled knowingly and nodded,

"Oh, it makes perfect sense," she agreed; I returned her smile and kept talking as if the joy found in the memory was spurring me on like an unseen force of energy.

"Anyway, it wasn't long before we were spending every moment we could together, exploring the world around us and sharing our thoughts and dreams. Being with him for the first time in my life, I felt a sense of ease and comfort. Wrapped in his arms, I had found my home, but it didn't last, and those comforting walls crumbled into dust, leaving me nowhere."

Hearing myself say those words aloud was overwhelming, from acknowledging the depth of my love for David to the boundless grief of his loss. Without warning, tears flowed while Athena May sat quietly, looking on with obvious concern, yet somehow, I could feel her warmth and comfort wrapping around my shoulders. After several minutes, the tidal wave that engulfed me finally retreated and left me exhausted, stranded on the beach of my emotions.

"I have to leave soon," Athena May said, glancing anxiously at the window, "Are you going to be alright, child?"

I nodded while quickly wiping my face on the edge of the blanket. After collecting her handbag, she rose from the armchair and looked intently at me,

"Are you sure?" she asked again.

"I might go home," I answered, "May I take your journal? I promise to be more careful."

The old lady nodded her agreement before saying she would leave the house first, just to ensure there were no police or any other unwelcome presence. Before waiting for me to agree, she hurried down the hallway and, without another word, was gone.

CHAPTER EIGHT

When I arrived back at my own home, the irony was not lost that every time I'd decided to leave it, somehow, I always ended up coming back. Something within these familiar walls was calling to me with a voice only heard by my subconscious. The motivation for this message was unknown to me, but I resolved to simply trust and wait for it to be revealed. I went straight to my room and typed the name 'Isabella Thorne' into my phone without pausing to do anything. After only a few seconds, several links appeared. I clicked on the first one, and the screen filled with a picture of a beautiful woman staring directly into the camera with an air of confidence that was almost tangible. A quick check of her profile and there was no question: it was the same person as that forceful girl from school. It came as no surprise to read that she was now working abroad for a civil rights organisation, and although it was undoubtedly pointless, I found myself apologising and wishing her well for the future. Feeling I had at least tried to properly acknowledge her place in my life, I switched off my phone and sank onto my bed. It felt like the right time to revisit the notebook again.

I found myself seated within what had resembled a vast, white bird resting with its wings outstretched when I'd first seen it from the airport window. But from that moment of pure awe, now we were poised for flight, and my fluttering heart was intoxicated by a vibrant

cocktail of excitement and trepidation. It had been nothing more than an idle fantasy for so long to actually visit a country that has only really been a part of my life through books. But having saved money in every possible way, I finally had enough to go, and with a boldness that surprised even me, I had just booked the trip with all the apparent confidence of a seasoned world traveller.

The cabin hummed as the passengers settled into their seats, their faces a medley of expressions - some weary just by the thought of the journey ahead, others were like me and brimming with wonder. As we waited, I thought of my parents, sadly both now passed, and allowed myself a moment to imagine their reaction. If I'd had the chance to tell them, I was going to fly in an aeroplane! My father would have offered stern warnings about the dangers while his eyes betrayed his apparent solemnity by twinkling with secret excitement.

As for my mother, I could picture her frowning, firmly reminding me that if humans were meant to fly, we would have been given wings.

Before I could think any more, the engines roared into life, and it felt like a low, rumbling vibration began to ripple through the plane; I gazed intently through the small oval window as the world outside blurred into a tapestry of colours that stretched beyond the horizon. The ground slowly surrendered to the inevitable, and I felt the weight of gravity release its hold.

The plane ascended, defying the boundaries of earth and sky, and through that same window, a breathtaking panorama unfolded before my eyes. Like cotton candy wisps, clouds were strung across the heavens while the radiant sun cast a boundless golden light.

As the plane soared even higher, I thought again about my fellow travellers. Here we were, strangers bound by a shared destination, representing all kinds of stories, dreams, and aspirations, coming from a multitude of backgrounds. But while sharing this plane, we were united, transcending all those barriers that might have divided us on the ground below.

The flight attendant glided down the narrow aisle, her voice an oasis of calm amid the hum of the engines. She

*offered a warm smile and reassurance, reminding the more
anxious passengers that we were in the hands of a highly
skilled team. As she effortlessly served refreshments
without appearing to even acknowledge the slight bumps of
turbulence.*

*After many hours, finally, the plane began its descent,
approaching the ground with gentle grace, and I braced
myself for landing. As the wheels touched the ground, some
around me visibly relaxed, expressing their gratitude for a
safe landing and jokingly stating it would be the last time
they would ever get a plane. But as I walked away from
that aircraft, I felt very differently. I'd always had a spirit
for adventure. Still, it was forever transformed by the wings
that had carried me to a place that had, until this moment,
been almost as mythical to me as Narnia or Avalon-Paris.
After checking into my small boutique hotel, I went straight
to the illustrious Champs-Élysées. Since I had first seen a
photograph many years ago, I had wondered what it would
be like to stand there. Now I was, and it was nothing less
than magical. The famous boulevard stretched before me
like a golden ribbon adorned with a thousand lights
threaded through the trees. Each one glowing, like tiny
golden beacons of all those dreams that were just like mine.*

It seemed as if the very essence of Paris flowed through its veins.

As I took my first step onto the wide promenade, a joyous symphony of footsteps and laughter greeted my senses. The air, brimming with the delicious scent of freshly baked pastries and heady aromas of strong coffee, spilt from the countless cafes, filled with people all seemingly speaking over each other with unrestrained excitement. All the while, the majestic Arc de Triomphe stood proudly at one end, looking down with the calm benevolence of a towering yet kindly deity. Bustling shops and chic boutiques beckoned with their elegant displays, each window a canvas of creativity and style.

As I continued my walk, the energy of the Champs-Élysées gradually infused me with every step. Couples strolled hand in hand, their love painted across their faces, while families gathered, their laughter echoing over the constant traffic noise. On such a sunny day, we all benefited from the welcome shade of the trees, their elegant branches gently curving towards the sky. Whichever direction I looked, the past seamlessly intertwined with the present; it was everything and so much more than even I could have imagined.

I was so moved by that first day I attended a lecture to learn more about both the city and the country. The speaker was a wise and learned individual with a deep understanding of the complexities of history and, perhaps, more importantly, the lessons it had to offer. As they spoke, I was struck by the power of their words. They spoke of the mistakes of the past, the triumphs, the tragedies, and the moments of great courage and resilience. They repeated the importance of understanding our shared history and how learning from the past could potentially create a better future. As they spoke, it was as if I was watching them carefully, gathering the threads of time and expertly weaving them together in a beautiful and profound way. Following the directions given to me by a young student who had been at the lecture, I wandered along cobbled streets, looking out for all the signs of the city's history held within the narrow alleyways. I imagined myself being there during all the most influential periods of history and hoped that I would have been as brave as those who had fought. I gazed up and saw the iconic Eiffel Tower through a gap between two houses. Until that moment, it had been hard to imagine how impressive it might be. Yet now, and despite my hope to appear a worldly and experienced traveller, I couldn't hide my disbelief that I was seeing it in person-it was breathtaking.

There was the same sense of awe when I stood on the bank of the River Seine, watching it flow gently beneath me, its waters mirroring the vibrant colours of the city. Illuminated boats cruised into the distance, negotiating the undulating contours of the river like attentive lovers caressing the soft curves of a woman. When I reached the Montmartre district, creativity seemed to be ingrained in the very fabric of the stone, as artists, both past and present, had unleashed their emotions onto canvas, their multicoloured hearts splashing vivid pigments onto the streets. I could almost picture Toulouse Lautrec heading to the Moulin Rouge, clutching a sketchbook, his mind filled with the anticipation of capturing the frenzy of pulsating desire as glorious women danced, throwing their many-layered skirts into the air before him. With every step I took, the rhythm of the French language embraced me, with each syllable sounding like a melody that I longed to understand. But I quickly realised the small phrase book I had bought from home was woefully inadequate to say anything other than a faltering 'Bonjour.'

After silently greeting the Mona Lisa at the Louvre, Le Jardin du Luxembourg beckoned me with its lavish greenery and tranquil beauty. I strolled beneath the trees and imagined they were whispering to me within their quivering leaves. Telling heartfelt tales of romance, where reckless lovers had found brief moments of solace in each other's arms amid the glorious flower beds and sun-kissed paths.

After enjoying coffee at a small cafe, I realised dusk was fast approaching, so I climbed the steps towards the glowing, angelic presence of the Sacré-Cœur Basilica. From this historic vantage point, Paris truly revealed its full beauty as the city lights flickered like twinkling, earthbound stars. I could hardly take in every detail of the breathtaking scene that stretched out before me, my heart swelling with gratitude for this opportunity to simply stand and stare- no longer trying to be anything other than myself. As I gazed out at the city, I wished I could go back, just for a moment, to that little girl in the country. Who spent her days daydreaming while kicking the dust in her hand-me-down shoes. I wish I could tell her what was to come.

Too soon, the time came for me to board a plane and head home. A studious-looking woman took her place next to me. After taking a book from her bag, she carefully stowed her belongings under the seat. She smiled at me and then settled back to read; despite being strangers, there was a sense of peace between us, which was most welcome amid the noise of some of the other passengers. There were raised voices from the back of the plane for a few minutes, but thankfully, once the engines roared into life, everyone calmed down, perhaps having realised there was no point in complaining anymore. I rested my head and thought back to Paris. It had been a truly magical experience, but there was no sadness about leaving. I knew whatever happened next, the city would always be with me. Sometime later, while still being lost in thought, I was startled by a voice beside me.

"It's amazing, isn't it?" the woman said, removing her glasses and gesturing towards the window, "to think that all this is just a speck in the universe. It really puts things into perspective."

I smiled in agreement, "It does; it should remind us all that we're all in this together, that our differences are small in the grand scheme of things."

The woman nodded thoughtfully, "Yes, and it makes you wonder what else is out there beyond our little planet. As it seems within a seemingly boundless universe, there must be other worlds like this one who might well wonder about us."

At that moment, our meals arrived, and as we ate, our conversation continued, sharing our knowledge with respect and genuine interest. After dinner and the cabin lights were dimmed, we fell back into a comfortable silence, and the plane continued its journey across the darkened ocean. When the plane finally touched down, as I gathered my things, my companion thanked me for making the flight such a pleasure, and I readily echoed my gratitude. We said our goodbyes, and I watched her hurry through the bustling airport before suddenly finding myself being swept up in the warm embrace of my friend, Catherine, who had come to welcome me home. We hugged tightly and immediately tried to catch up on all that had happened since we last saw each other. I babbled almost incoherently about Paris while she shared all the latest gossip from work, openly relishing the more salacious rumours which reduced me to helpless laughter.

As the car pulled up, I was welcomed by the familiar sight of my little home, with its brick walls and wooden shutters. The front yard was packed with roses, daisies, and all the other flowers I had carefully raised. As I walked amongst them, their heads bobbed excitedly as if happy I had come back, and my lungs gratefully breathed in the fresh air, which erased the memory of the slight staleness of being on the plane.

Inside, every room was filled with the warm glow of the afternoon sun. I could hear the sound of birds singing outside and the gentle tinkling of the wind chimes by the back door, which somehow always managed to rise above the constant low hum of the traffic. It was as if the house itself was alive, welcoming me back with open arms. Catherine and I were hungry after the long journey, and we decided to head to a local fish restaurant that the local news had been raving about for weeks. As we walked in, the smell of freshly cooked seafood filled my nostrils, and my mouth began to water with anticipation. We were greeted by a friendly server who showed us to our table, and we avidly studied the menu, trying to decide what to order. Catherine almost immediately chose the fish and chips, but I decided to try the grilled salmon with roasted vegetables. When our food arrived, it looked and smelled divine. We chatted and laughed as we ate, enjoying each other's company and savouring every bite of the delicious food. After finishing our main meal, we jokingly decided that having a dessert would be greedy while immediately ordering a decadent chocolate cake with a scoop of vanilla ice cream. It was the perfect ending to a wonderful meal, *and we left the restaurant feeling very full but, more importantly, completely content.*

As we walked out into the evening air, I couldn't help but feel grateful for the simple pleasures in life - good food, good company, and the joy of discovering new places and experiences.

Later that evening, as I sat on the couch, sipping a cup of tea, my mind began to wander, reflecting on the journey that had brought me here. I thought back to my childhood days, filled with laughter and innocence. I remembered my family, all the wonderful friends and lovers, each one either being a part of a joyous memory or a painful lesson I had needed to learn along the way. Who would have believed all that would happen? Owning my own home and having a job that I not only enjoyed but also gave me the resources to travel to places that had been nothing more than pictures in a book. I wanted to think for longer, but when the weariness of the long day refused to be ignored, I wandered to bed, knowing I would dream.

I carefully placed the notebook on my bedside table and rested back on my pillow. David and I had also gone to Paris many years later. Although it was still as stunning as Athena May had described, we witnessed political unrest and protest marches, highlighting what appeared to be a growing dissatisfaction with life itself within the majority of the population. But for all the differences between her experience in the city and mine, there was one thing on which we could agree. At its best, Paris is an undeniably special place. As she carried some of its magic with her, so did I. However, somehow, amid the chaos of my mind, it had become lost. But as was now becoming apparent, Athena May could find those pockets of light within the darkness and make them glow brighter again.

With all this talk of the past, I foolishly allowed myself to drift back and, within moments, profoundly negative thoughts and long-held doubts crowded me, pushing and shoving their way to the front, demanding to be heard. Somehow, all those words about finding kindness had been written on nothing more than a faint mist that was easily burned away by the harsh cruelty of my own mind. How I wished things had been different if only a mere twist of fate could have altered the course of events. How I could feel that my heart still carried the weight of regret, a burden that seemed to grow heavier with every passing day. Memories danced like cruel shadows, each one a malevolent reminder of the choices made and the roads not taken. In desperation, I clamped my hands to the side of my head in a vain attempt to shut everything out. But the echoes of mocking laughter and the haunted cries of lost love still managed to make their presence felt, now mingling with all those missed opportunities that somehow left an unmistakably bitter taste on my tongue.

It seemed however hard I tried to look forward, the past was always going to be there like an angry spirit refusing to release me from its control. I knew there was no denying I longed for a second chance, to hold tighter to all those dreams I had shared with David that had somehow slipped through my fingers like grains of sand. I would do anything to be able to rewind the clock because then I could have made him proud of me. Wherever he was now, he would have seen his spirit was alive in me, experiencing everything in his name.

But life, as I had come to learn, was not a dazzling mosaic of wishes fulfilled. It was an intricate tapestry of choices and consequences, interwoven with the unpredictable threads of chance. I couldn't escape the reality that unfolded before me nor rewrite the chapters that had already been written. The past was etched in stone, indelible and unyielding.

I began to feel the overwhelming sense of hopelessness that regularly pervaded my thoughts. But just as I started to slip into accepting that even trying to live was always going to be a futile effort, I felt something change deep within me. As I lay there, with my eyes tightly closed, I started to see a tiny yet stubborn light fiercely burning, defiantly confronting the creeping darkness. I focused all my attention on its persistent flame until it started to slowly spread, much as the sun's rays of dawn might steal from the night. Even though I was well aware it was undoubtedly a product of my imagination, it felt like it was a sign, reminding me of everything Athena May had written or said since we had met. As I stared intently, a small voice spoke, urging me to find solace in the present and to make peace with the ghosts of what could have been. Despite what I had come to believe, it insisted there were still opportunities to learn from the roads not taken.

Suddenly feeling unnerved by what was happening, I pulled my hands away from my head and opened my eyes as wide as possible. I quickly reassured myself it was probably nothing more than a hallucination brought about by tiredness or, more likely, the fact that I had missed taking my medication. Without pausing to question, I leapt up and raced to the bathroom, stopping only to grab the pill bottle. I practically threw them into my mouth and then splashed my face with cold water.

After taking a few deep breaths, I went back to the bedroom and, after straightening the discarded sheets, settled back into bed. Not having any idea of what the time might be, I pulled the covers over me and acknowledged that even trying to think about the future was exhausting, it was as unknown and as potentially perilous as what might lie in the depths of the deepest oceans. It had always terrified me, and now, the prospect of facing it was overwhelming. So, it was no surprise my mind was having such incredible difficulty trying to think about it. But as my eyelids started to droop, thanks to the effects of the medication, my last thought was more unexpected than any of the others that had taken up permanent residence in my mind. Supposing I had been wrong, and I wasn't alone? Wouldn't that make it so much easier? Knowing that whatever might happen, someone-maybe even David-would be there with me? As I consciously made some space for this thought to grow, for the first time in what seemed like forever, I truly started to understand what Athena May had spoken about with such certainty.

CHAPTER NINE

Hours later, I awoke to the gentle rays of sunlight filtering through my curtains, casting delicate patterns on the walls. After less than a minute of simply appreciating the soft light, the silence was abruptly broken by a dull thud, as if something had fallen from the top of the wardrobe. At first, I wondered whether I had knocked something off the bedside table, but as I tried to blink away the remnants of sleep, my eyes focused on an unexpected sight that left me momentarily breathless. Standing at the foot of my bed was a young woman unlike anyone I had ever seen before. Her presence was striking, her aura demanding attention. Clad in a close-fitting, cornflower blue dress that accentuated her curves, she exuded confidence and a sense of self-assuredness. Every slight movement she made seemed deliberate, and her heavy makeup, carefully applied, seemed too much for someone so young and yet somehow, on her face, it worked and added a sense of adult knowing to her apparent innocence.

Still half asleep at first, my dazed mind tried to make some sense of how she had got here. But thankfully, a logical explanation eventually found its way through, and I simply questioned whether she was even real or merely a figment of my imagination, a creation of a dream that had lingered far too long into the waking hours. I rubbed my eyes, half-hoping that this was all nothing more than a hallucination. But despite my efforts, when I dared to look again, there was no need for further debate as she was most definitely there.

As our eyes met, I glimpsed a hint of pure vulnerability hidden within her gaze that seemed at odds with her seductive appearance. Without uttering a word, she turned and gracefully walked towards the window, her high heels making no discernible noise on the wooden floor. I watched as she stood there, peering out at the world beyond. The cityscape sprawled before her, and, for a moment, she seemed almost surprised to see what was there.

Not knowing quite what to say or do, I stayed silent and just watched her silhouette etched against the sunlit backdrop of the city's skyline. I couldn't help but wonder what was going through her mind. There was something wistful in her expression, a definite melancholy that prevented me from being too abrupt when asking why she was there. At last, she turned to face me and, still without speaking, settled into the chair in the corner of my room.

"I thought it was time I visited with you again," she began, seeing me frown, she laughed, throwing her head back, her hair tumbling like waves over her slim shoulders. Now completely confused, I drew back the covers and looked again at her. Sure, I had never seen this woman before in my life.

"We've met?" I stammered as my brain frantically searched through the myriad of images in my memory.

"Don't you recognise me?" She persisted in her playful tone in sharp contrast to the intense look in her large eyes. On acknowledging my still blank expression, she reached into the pocket of her dress, pulled out a rainbow ball, and tossed it into the air only to catch it in her perfectly manicured hand.

"That's Miss Elizabeth's ball," I said as if speaking more with myself than anyone else.

"So the fact I have it means?" she asked, cocking her head to one side.

"You know her?" I replied weakly.

Frustrated with what seemed like my deliberate stupidity, she abruptly threw the ball towards me.

"I am her," she snapped.

I caught the ball and looked back at her; it couldn't be possible! This young woman was at least sixteen or seventeen years old, whereas Miss Elizabeth was a child. There had to be some mistake; perhaps this was a prank, or

I was having some kind of mental breakdown. Seemingly oblivious to the effect she was having on my psyche, she sighed heavily and leaned back in the chair. There was a distinctly uneasy silence between us for several moments until I finally remembered how to speak and asked why she was there. My words came out of my mouth with an uncharacteristic bluntness, which caused her to immediately straighten up and glare back at me.

"I came because I know you've been talking with Athena May, so I thought you might want to talk to me too, but just like always, it looks like I was wrong," she said petulantly, "I know it's because I'm not like her. All the time, growing up, it was always why can't you be more like your sister? She always says and does the right thing, so why can't you be more like her, Ellie?"

Although her distaste for this memory was abundantly clear, one word stood out for me way above all the others.

"Sister?" I gasped, "You're Ellie, Athena May's sister?"

Her sulky expression changed; she rolled her eyes and sighed again.

"Well, obviously," she replied sarcastically, "you're not very smart, are you?"

As I felt I owed it to Athena May, I opted to ignore her unpleasant attitude and instead said what a genuine pleasure it was to meet her finally.

"I've read so much about you," I gushed while some small part of my mind was still trying to work out how this young woman and the little girl could be the same person. My enthusiasm clearly pleased her as she visibly relaxed, a broad smile lightening her whole face.

"I loved learning about your childhood, your parents and those trips to see your grandmother," I continued, "she sounds like an extraordinary woman."

"Yes, she was," Ellie replied quickly, "but what about when I got older? Is that in the book, too?"

I thought for a moment and shook my head, but as soon as I saw her expression change back to frustrated petulance, I quickly assured her that I hadn't read the whole book yet. But Ellie simply scowled and shook her head with evident disgust,

"Of course, I'm not mentioned," she muttered angrily, "Nothing changes, does it? She always has to be seen in the best light, in front of everything. While the real truth and I are hidden somewhere in the background."

Without waiting for me to speak, she stood up and strode fiercely across the bedroom, pausing at the door to look back at me. I expected her to say something filled with some level of anger that would match her apparent irritation. But instead, she smiled sweetly, and in a voice that sounded like soft caramel, Ellie spoke again,

"Anyway, next time you see my sister, make sure you ask about Cal Mulvane, as I'm sure when you've heard that part of the story, you'll see Miss Athena May Bower very differently."

I stood up from my bed and started towards her, but Ellie spun on her heel and hurried downstairs without a backward glance before she could discern even the slightest movement in my body. I went to follow her but tripped over my discarded shoes, and by the time I had regained my balance, I reached the door. Somehow, I knew, even without looking, she wouldn't be there.

After quickly straightening up the bedclothes, I grabbed the notebook and scanned the pages, but it seemed there was no mention of the name. Even after checking twice more, Cal Mulvane appeared nowhere within the pages. I rested the closed book on my lap and tried to think about what had just happened, but whatever solution came to mind, it had all the permanence of a nervous butterfly flitting amongst lavender. No idea took root as none of them made any logical sense. At last, I resolved to read more of the notebook and hoped, at some stage, it would either bring some much-needed clarity or, at the very least, distract me until I felt able to go back to Athena May's house. My first instinct had been to go there immediately, but Ellie's tone when she'd mentioned the name had unnerved me, so it felt best to try and learn more before raising what could be an unhappy topic for Athena May. She had been so kind and patient with me, and I didn't want to cause her any distress. So I wandered downstairs and sank into the couch, the house around me was shrouded in a protective silence. Outside, everyone was going about their business with all the associated noise and chaos, yet these familiar walls kept me safe and hidden from it all. Over the years, every therapist proclaimed the alleged joys of playing an active role in that world, but they failed to understand how that notion filled me with crippling dread. I knew I didn't belong there. Determined to push those all too familiar thoughts from my mind before they could take hold, I forcibly turned all my attention back to the notebook. There were now even more questions than before, so I hoped to find some answers.

When I met Ellie from the train, she was dressed in her best clothes, clutching her small suitcase and wearing a floral

scarf around her neck that I knew belonged to our mother.
When we stepped outside the station, she looked exactly
what she was: a young woman from the country with wide
eyes that eagerly drank in everything with unfettered
excitement. I could almost hear her heart quickening,
racing to keep time with the rhythm of the vibrant streets
that stretched out like veins, pulsating with life. I was so
happy she had finally come to visit. There were so many
things I wanted to share with her, but I had no way of
knowing just how quickly the city would completely engulf
her senses.

Having lived here for a couple of years, it was wonderful to
be reminded of the sheer wonder of seeing it all for the first
time. I noticed things again that had become almost
invisible to me: the tall buildings soaring above us,
reaching for the heavens with their metallic spires, casting
long shadows on the crowded sidewalks below. The
cacophony of car horns, the ceaseless chatter of voices and
the air tinged with wafts of roasted coffee intermingled with
the sharp tang of car exhausts.

When we got back to my home, I had imagined we would sit
and talk, but Ellie was bristling with energy, fidgeting to be
out the door again and soaking everything in as if she only
had a few precious moments instead of the promised week.

She was clearly dazzled by the cityscape, speaking at double speed, her mouth trying to keep up with every sight that caught her eyes. More than once, she was almost seduced by the neon signs that flickered and beckoned, promising dubious pleasures and illicit delights. I found myself having to take a firm grip on her arm and lead her away, only to be halted again as she gazed into shop windows that contained displays that must have seen to her like rare treasures from a faraway land. Sometimes, she gasped with pure delight, whereas there were other moments when her innocent expression seemed to change into one of pure lust. She would rest her fingers on the glass as if this action would bring her closer to the object of desire while murmuring all its apparent attributes to herself. At one particular jewellery store, it was almost impossible to tear her away from the display; her eyes glowed with white fire.

"Can you imagine having one of those on your finger?" she asked, pointing at an especially large ring encrusted with diamonds. Without waiting for me to answer, she continued, "If I had one, I would never take it off."

"But what about when you were washing dishes?" I replied, vainly hoping to wake my sister from her daydream.

"I wouldn't be washing dishes or doing any kind of housework," she answered firmly, "No, Athena May, my days would be about fancy restaurants, wearing fine clothes while my staff would take care of the house."

I laughed and gently tugged at her arm,

"Well, until that happens, Ellie, there's much more for you to see."

As the day wore on, even though I was starting to get weary, I held onto her, completely charmed by her passionate excitement and loving her joyful laughter. For all her wild aspirations, being with her was like having a piece of home with me again, and so however many streets she wished to wander down, I was delighted to be her guide.

But after those first few glorious days, I noticed a change in her. It was barely noticeable at first, but then it emerged: a comment or a look started to betray the fact that she was far from happy when comparing my life to her own. On one particular afternoon, what felt like her envy finally showed itself.

"Your life has everything," she began, "you have all the excitement and possibilities, whereas I'm stuck in the middle of nowhere with nothing. It's not fair! Why should you have all of this? Why can't I have my share, too?"

At first, I tried to patiently explain that I only had my home because I worked hard and made sacrifices. Still, she dismissively waved away what felt like a perfectly reasonable explanation.

"Work? That's all you do, Athena May. You're wasting your time. No, if I lived here, I would be out every night, drinking champagne and dancing all night in one of those rooftop places that overlook the city."

"And how would you pay for all this fancy living?" my tone was laced with far more sarcasm than I had intended. But instead of reacting as I'd expected with either a pout or her deciding to flounce out of the room dramatically. Ellie turned and smiled at me, but not with pleasure; it was in a way that made me feel very unnerved.

"Oh, I wouldn't be paying for anything. I've been thinking about it since I got here; what I need to do is find myself a nice rich man, and then I can have anything I want."

For a moment, I could almost hear our mother rebuking her for having such an idea. But as she wasn't with us, all I could do was try and assume some kind of parental role. So I shook my head at what sounded like nothing more than a fantasy, adding that I couldn't see why anyone would just give someone so much without getting anything in return. Ellie looked away and walked over to the window, and she gazed out; her reply, when it came, took me entirely by surprise.

"All I have to do is find out what he'd want and then give it to him," she replied thoughtfully.

I didn't forget her remark, and despite still feeling decidedly uncomfortable, I finally gave in to her incessant pleas and promised to take her to a nightclub. It seemed harmless enough, after all, she could hardly make a habit out of going, as she was due to go home again in a few days. Also, I'd thought about what she'd said about me having so much. I had to admit to myself that perhaps I had started to take it all for granted. So I agreed we could go, and the sheer joy on Ellie's face as she flung her arms around my neck filled me with so much pleasure my doubts about the wisdom of this particular excursion faded into the background. But with the benefit of hindsight, I should have listened to those doubts.

I will never forget the first time I encountered Cal Mulvane, until that fateful night, it was a name only ever whispered through the shadows of the city. By all accounts, just being in his presence was described as being in the middle of a tempestuous storm while a swirl of deceit and danger clung to him like an invisible cloak. From the moment our paths

166

collided, I could almost sense the murky depths of his involvement in criminal activities.

Cal possessed the aura of a man who had danced with darkness and embraced its treacherous charms. His coal-black eyes, framed by artfully- curved eyebrows, glinted like shards of broken glass, flickering as they observed everything in his immediate vicinity. His thin lips were twisted into a perpetual smirk, but when they did separate, rows of perfect white teeth were revealed, like an alligator smile. He spoke in a soft, low tone that oozed with snake-like charm, somehow being both threatening and seductive in equal measure. That night, when he sauntered into the club, just his presence commanded attention. As I watched, there was no question he drew both fear and fascination from all who dared to look at him. He wore a dark-coloured, tailored suit with thin, crisp lapels resembling two razor-sharp blades angled across his broad chest. A black silk tie highlighted his gleaming, high-buttoned white shirt, and as he walked, the arrow-straight creases in his trousers barely moved other than to graze the tops of his highly polished shoes. His appearance exuded an air of reckless rebellion., yet he also openly relished the overly respectful niceties of the nightclub owner who fawned over him, snapping fingers at staff, ordering only the best for this honoured yet dishonourable guest.

Whenever his name had been mentioned to me, particularly by the men in the office, it was always whispered in hushed tones, their eyes filled with a strange mix of admiration and caution. They spoke of his involvement in illicit trades, deals made in the dead of night and fortunes amassed through every possible crime. It is no exaggeration to say his name had become synonymous with danger. So when I finally saw this man, it was like I was in the presence of a legend, someone who it seemed couldn't possibly exist anywhere other than in a crime novel.

I watched as he was ushered to a booth, where a martini was already waiting for him, delivered by an attractive showgirl dressed in full costume. Despite her effort to move closer to him, he barely acknowledged her presence, choosing to focus his attention on the conversation of his two male companions. As I watched, I couldn't help but wonder if, beneath the veneer of his criminal exploits, there was just an ordinary man who had become trapped in the clutches of his own fearsome reputation. My thoughts were interrupted by the excited chatter of my sister.

Since she had arrived in the city, Ellie had ravenously devoured every experience with all the intensity of a caged

creature that had suddenly found itself free. So now, sitting
in a nightclub, even though she was only drinking a Coke,
the thrill of it all was almost tangible for her.

"Who is he?" she asked, looking eagerly across the
crowded room, her young face beaming with undiluted
pleasure.

"I believe that's Cal Mulvane," I replied, quickly adding,
"I don't know him; I've just seen his picture in the
newspapers."

"He's just so impressive, like a real-life movie star," Ellie
sighed, sipping her drink.

"He's no movie star, Ellie," I continued, "they say he's a
dangerous man."

I had hoped my words would sound like a warning to my
young sister, but instead, she just leaned forward slightly
and stared even more intently at him. Somehow, despite the
nightclub owner's near-constant attention and the other
patrons' curious glances, Cal noticed my sister and sent
drinks over to our table, smiling when he saw them arrive
and her delighted reaction. Ignoring my insistence that she
was too young, Ellie sipped the cocktail and managed not
to grimace at the unfamiliar, bitter taste. Believing I
needed to maintain a clear head, I left mine untouched. I
tried to engage her in conversation, but Ellie did little more

than nod a vague acknowledgement as she gazed unashamedly at Cal, her face breaking into a broad smile every time their eyes met. At last, he rose and strolled to our table, the crowded dance floor parting like the Red Sea before Moses and stretched his hand towards Ellie.

"Of all the women here tonight, you are the most beautiful. May I ask you to dance?" he asked, slightly bowing his head. My sister took his hand, and before I had a chance to object, they had left me behind and were now in the centre of the room, gently swaying to the soft blues being played by the band.

As I looked on, in the depths of my soul, an unsettling thought took root, unfurling its tendrils with a mix of disbelief and anguish. It was something I had never anticipated, a revelation that pierced through the fabric of all my so-called wisdom. With all her innocence and purity, my younger sister willingly became entangled in a web spun by Cal Mulvane. The weight of this knowledge settled upon my shoulders, burdening me with a sense of responsibility and protectiveness. How did this happen? Now their paths had crossed, there wasn't a doubt in my troubled mind that he would lead her down a road paved with danger.

*He dominated her attention for the remainder of the
evening, plying her with drinks and becoming ever closer
and more intimate with every dance. Much to my relief, he
finally ushered her back to our table and apologised
profusely for taking up so much of her time.*

*"I'm afraid I have to leave you, lovely ladies; I have a
business meeting to attend."*

*He smiled at me, and when I made no effort to respond, he
quickly turned his attention back to Ellie, kissing her hand
while looking into her eyes with blatant longing.*

*"I will see you again very soon," he said firmly before
turning away and leaving the nightclub, with his two
companions rushing to follow him like obedient dogs
following their master.*

*Over the next few days, I barely saw Ellie and had to make
a series of feeble excuses to those back home who were
waiting for her to return. One morning, I finally caught up
with her when she sleepily emerged from the bedroom, still
with the smudged remnants of makeup that had been
applied the previous night.*

*"Don't you think things are moving a little fast?" I began
tentatively, trying to sound as casual as possible.*

"Better than not moving at all," replied Ellie, "all you ever do is work and pay bills, don't you ever just want to have some fun?"

Before I had a chance to answer, she took my arm and forced me to sit down at the kitchen table, and for a moment, she looked like a wide-eyed young girl again.

"Come to dinner with us tonight, Athena May. A whole load of us are going, and it'll give you a chance to get to know Cal. Not the person they talk about in the news, he told me himself that's all just exaggeration, but the real man."

Seeing my reluctance, she took my hand in her own, "Please come, just give him a chance," she pleaded. Despite all my misgivings, I heard myself agreeing, and Ellie gleefully flung her arms around my neck. "You won't regret it!" she exclaimed.

That night, I found myself in one of the city's most exclusive restaurants; as before, the staff treated Cal like royalty. At the table, when he told a joke, everyone laughed, they ate when he did and eagerly toasted him at every possible moment. But I wasn't so lost in his seductive magic, as I saw in his company, my sister had changed. The innocence that once defined her was now tinged with a hint of rebellion, a fire ignited by the dangerous liaison they shared. Her eyes sparkled with a mixture of passion and vulnerability, and it became increasingly obvious their relationship had become overtly sexual. I carefully watched them together as I tried to come to terms with this new reality. Very occasionally, it seemed there might just be more to Cal Mulvane's character than I had anticipated. Despite his enigmatic charm, there appeared to be flickers of tenderness in his gaze as he looked at Ellie, a genuine affection that seemed to transcend the darkness that surrounded him. It was a bittersweet moment, for I knew that my sister had found solace in the arms of a man undoubtedly capable of both love and destruction.

In the face of this revelation, I wrestled with conflicting emotions. As the protective older sister, my primary desire was to shield my sister from what seemed like the inevitable heartache that awaited her. But I had also long believed in the power of love and vainly hoped it might be capable of softening even the most hardened souls. I constantly found myself torn between intervening and standing aside, but this was Ellie, so I had no option but to be there for her and just see how things turned out.

With every passing week, their relationship grew more entangled in a dance of passion and danger. With a mix of trepidation and hope, I watched while openly lying to

everyone back home that Ellie had found a job and would
be staying much longer than initially planned. Her small
closet overflowed with dresses, gowns, shoes and
accessories, each one probably costing more than my
week's salary. With all the bright-eyed excitement of a
child at Christmas, Ellie would show me her latest gift from
Cal. She would hold up each piece of jewellery and watch it
sparkle, relishing its beauty while willingly surrendering to
every sensory pleasure its possession gave her.

But while she talked dreamily of getting engaged and
maybe even married, as I had feared, Cal had a very
different future planned. It was late afternoon when one of
his men knocked at the door. Without even attempting to
spare her feelings, he dismissively announced the
relationship was over and that Cal didn't want to see her
anymore. She was welcome to keep his gifts but was to
make no further contact with him. As quickly as he had
picked her up, Cal Mulvane ruthlessly discarded Ellie, like
an unwanted trinket that had been briefly diverting but was
now a source of boredom for him.

As the door closed, my sister's fragile heart shattered into
a thousand pieces, scattering all her dreams and hopes.
The love she had been convinced was unbreakable
crumbled beneath the weight of his callousness, leaving her

abandoned, lost in the rubble. I wanted to say something, anything that could ease her intense pain, but my words went unheard as she retreated into her room. Later that night, when I heard her sobbing, I tapped on the door, but as I turned the handle, it became apparent it was locked. I sat at the kitchen table, my mind a mass of confusion and uncommon rage at this man who had hurt my sister so badly. At one point, I even contemplated going out and finding him, demanding he come and see her, but I knew it would be a pointless effort. Trying to distract myself, I flipped open the unread newspaper only to see a picture of Cal with his arm around a glamorous showgirl- maybe even the one who had been there that first night, but I wasn't sure. I quickly threw the paper away, knowing it could only cause Ellie more distress.

The following morning, both of us were exhausted from the sleepless night and sat in silence at the table until I plucked up the courage to suggest maybe it was time for Ellie to go home.

"Maybe in a day or so," she replied faintly. I tried to convince myself she was considering the idea as I got ready for work. More than once, I suggested it would be best if I stayed home as I didn't want to leave her alone, but she insisted that it would be fine. It was early evening when I

arrived home, and it was immediately obvious she had found comfort in the arms of a different kind of companion. Ellie was slumped on the sofa by her side; a half-empty bottle stood on the floor, and a glass rested on her chest, held in place by her hand. The pungent scent of alcohol filled the air, mingling with her tears and with each sip, I could see she was hoping to drown the pain that threatened to consume her, to numb the ache that gnawed at her heart. She squinted up at me as I edged closer,

"Are you alright?" I asked while tentatively reaching for the glass, but before my fingers had even touched the drink, she angrily pulled it away and drained every drop. Without speaking, she rose unsteadily to her feet and glared at me before picking up the bottle and wandering into her room, slamming the door behind her. I sat at the kitchen table and tried to decide what to do while glancing at the bedroom and straining to hear even the slightest sound. After what felt like hours, I tiptoed and pressed my ear to the door, but there was nothing. Despite knowing it would probably irritate Ellie, I knocked and called out her name, but the only response was a low moan and a slurred order to leave her alone. I briefly considered making some dinner, but it felt pointless, so, finally, I wandered into my own room and prayed that in the morning, the worst would be over.

But it was not to be. As the days passed, I watched helplessly as her spirit spiralled downward, becoming increasingly lost in a labyrinth of self-destruction. She rapidly became a mere shadow of herself, haunted by the memories of a love that, perhaps only in her mind, had slipped through her fingers like fine sand. I racked my brains, still desperately trying to think of anything that might help, longing to pull her back from the edge of her despair. On the rare occasions when she appeared more reasonable, I would plead with her to seek help or alternatively be stern, ordering her to pull herself together, telling her that no man was worth falling apart over. But whatever I said and in whatever tone, my futile efforts were always met with the same glassy, lifeless stare as if Ellie's soul was no longer present in her body. I quickly learned that addiction is a relentless enemy that clings to its victims with a seemingly unbreakable determination. And so, most of the time, I found myself to be nothing more than a concerned but ultimately useless bystander.

But then, when it had seemed things couldn't get any worse, I came home from work to find Ellie collapsed on the bathroom floor, drenched in a thick pool of blood. In a blind panic, I flew to the phone and called an ambulance before racing back to her side, completely convinced she had tried to commit suicide. I clutched her hands in mine and prayed with every ounce of my heart for her to survive, making reckless promises to the divine if only my dear sister could be spared. But when the medical team arrived, it didn't take long for them to ascertain, to my abject horror, that she had miscarried. Ellie had been pregnant with Cal's child all this time, and I hadn't known. I had been so blind, failing to see what was right in front of me. For days and nights, I didn't move from her bedside and simply watched her sleep, crippled with guilt for my own failing. Finally, Ellie was deemed well enough to be discharged from the hospital, but another shock was in store when I came to collect her. Walking into her room, she was already dressed, her clothes hanging from her fragile frame and her face still showing the emotional scars of everything she had lost. Before I could speak, Ellie announced a cab had been booked that would take her to the station.

"I'm going home, Athena May," she said simply, "I'm sure that will make you happy, as that's what you've wanted all along."

I stood there, utterly speechless, as she continued to explain that it was clear I had never liked Cal, and perhaps if I had been more welcoming to him, their relationship *might have worked out. She spoke with icy formality about how I had made no effort to understand the depth of their feelings for each other.*

"But in your mind, you probably felt there was no need to try because, whatever the situation, you always know best, don't you? Ever since we were children, it's been the same. Well, this time, you were wrong, Athena May, more wrong than you have ever been in your whole life."

I opened my mouth to speak, but Ellie had already picked up her bag and appeared to be walking out the door without even the slightest hesitation. But then she stopped and looked at me with more pity in her eyes than anger.

"I feel truly sorry for you because for all your books, for all that fine education, you will never know what it means to love someone other than yourself."

I half-ran after her, pleading to be heard, but it was as if she had become deaf and so kept walking away. I reached the main hospital doors just in time to see her get into the taxi, which quickly disappeared into the traffic. Ellie was gone because I had failed.

A friend from home called the following day to say my sister had arrived safely home and asked what had happened. Not knowing what to say, I muttered something vague about city life not suiting her. Over the following

*weeks, I wrote countless letters. Still, when they were all
returned unopened, I finally stopped and forced myself to
try and be content with the knowledge that, at least, she
was surrounded by family and friends who would help her
fully recover. As the passage of time was to prove, I was
very much mistaken about that, too.*

*Although, over time, the pain of what happened became
less raw, there was no doubt I would always carry shame
for what happened with Ellie. For months after we parted, I
awoke each morning burdened by the weight of guilt that
clung to my soul. The memory of letting her down, my dear
sister, haunted me, permeating every breath I took. So
many times, I found myself wishing there was a way to
rewrite the past as the shadows of regret danced before my
eyes, mocking my inability to turn back time. On my darkest
days, I relived that time in my mind, cursing myself for not
acting differently, for not being stronger and for not
understanding the depth of my sister's pain until it was too
late. If a lesson were to be learned, it would come at a very
high price.*

*At last, after much painfully difficult introspection, a day
dawned when it felt that it was time to try and move
forward, but not before making a solemn vow. I swore that
I would try always to be more mindful of the suffering of*

others, to fight but with loving compassion and not self-opinionated judgment. But most importantly of all, I would never allow anyone to fall again.

I slowly closed the book and sighed heavily; now I knew that's why Athena May had been there for me. At that moment, without even the vaguest idea of the time, I knew I had to go back to her house.

CHAPTER TEN

I stepped out into the street, gasping slightly when a sudden icy touch trailed down my neck, a breath from an impossible winter. My heart thudded in my chest, quicker to see the danger than my eyes. There was a man. Against the unforgiving light of the streetlamp, he was little more than a silhouette, features obscured by the harsh light and deeper shadow. I stiffened, feet refusing to move any further. His presence was palpable, and I shivered as goosebumps prickled on my arms and neck. How did it feel so cold? And how was it so silent? I could only hear my shallow breaths and the dull rhythm of my heart as it beat against my chest as if aching to escape.

The silhouette was so still I could almost pretend it was a statue or just a trick of the light. Yet it was watching me, I could feel its gaze like a physical touch on my skin. It wasn't a curious stare or even an admiring one- it felt like the eyes of a predator. How a snake gazes, motionless from the forest floor, at the helpless mouse, who is frozen by fear. Squinting, I tried to see its face, yet the light from behind was too bright and the night too dark; I could barely make out the outline of a long coat draping over the tall figure. My muscles tensed, begging me to run, yet the figure moved just when I took a step. A tilt of the head allowed the streetlamps to catch his eyes; they reflected at me with cool amusement. My body went limp, the tension draining from me, replaced by an odd weakness. If I tried to take a step, I'd crumple to the floor, and a part of me wondered if I could stand again. His eyes were unblinking, and I shivered again. It felt as though they could see through me, past my face and into my heart, into every wound, every scar. He tilted his head again, and somehow, I felt I'd been deemed lacking. There was no warmth, just a sunless cold. Ice buried far beneath the sun, never touched by light- instead left to grow into something bitter and unforgiving.

I still couldn't move and tried curling my clammy hands into weak fists while feebly coaxing my legs into running back into the house. Away from whatever, whoever was lingering in the dark. It took everything to lift my foot, but then, to my horror, I realised I'd somehow stepped towards the figure. His gaze didn't change, the light reflecting off his eyes like blackened glass.

He tilted his head again, the flash of white teeth glinting in the streetlamp's glow. I swallowed, wondering how a smile could look so much more like an animal baring its fangs. Why wasn't I running? A tiny part of my brain screamed at me. Yet, it was utterly overshadowed by a different, intensely confusing impulse to lean slightly closer, to touch the blade's edge and feel the burning ice.

"Hello."

His snake-like voice sent fresh shivers through me, every word cool and sharp, carrying the promise of venom.

"If I may ask, where are you rushing off to in such a hurry?" He asked, and while his tone was one of refined politeness, it did nothing to quell the fear in my veins. I shuddered, torn between wanting to move closer and wanting to run, yet a single bright thought blazed through my mind: why all of this felt familiar.

"Mr. Mulvane," I exhaled shakily, knowing it was impossible but undeniably true.

He inclined his head,

"It is always nice to be recognised." He replied, straightening once again, "especially after all this time- it is gratifying to know I am remembered." His eyes gleamed in the dark.

It felt as if I'd slipped into a nightmare.

"I believe," Cal continued, an edge creeping into the politeness, "I asked you a question. Where are you going?" I forced myself to inhale, to lift my chin and meet his inhuman stare,

"I don't believe that's any of your business." I replied, trying to match his cool politeness, before a spark of my own reignited, "And not to argue, but you are only remembered by a few. To the rest of the world? You're utterly insignificant."

His smile vanished, and his eyes grew hollow until it felt like I was peering into a dark abyss. A shudder rippled through me, and I instantly regretted my words. The spark that had flickered to life now felt smothered by the cold shadows.

"Either way," I managed, this time my voice sounded thin, "I have to go," while forcing my stiff legs into cooperation so I could walk past him. Yet before I could take another step, pain lanced through my arm. With a gasp, I pulled up my sleeve, only to see what looked like an oil stain spreading over the skin, black serpentine coils curled around my arm. My skin stung where they touched like scalding ice had leached into my bones.

"Now, let's not be rude. I've never been one to abide bad manners."

I swallowed a whimper, the pain sending small, black splotches over my eyes.

I forced the apology out of chattering teeth before stammering, "What... What do you want?"

The pain lessened slightly, although the oily black tendrils didn't fade from my skin.

"That's better. I expected more from you, Jenna. May I call you Jenna? It feels only fair as you know my name."

I nodded, and he smiled, his perfectly straight teeth glinting with his obvious amusement.

"Now, before you were so rude, I was simply going to ask you to pass on a message." I blinked,

"A message?" I repeated,

He inclined his head, and in a hazy blur of fractured shadows, he moved to be in front of me. Being so close, I could see he was breathtakingly handsome, in the same lethal way a knife can seem beautiful in the moonlight.

"A message… to Athena May Bower." He said, her name sounding like a curse in his cold voice. His pleasant mask seemed to falter for a moment, and I saw a distorted rage twist his fine features.

"What's the message?" I asked, voice barely a whisper.

"She is going to learn the price of lying." He replied, his eyes boring into mine, unblinking and furious, "She is going to feel the consequences of writing such blatant slander about me." His thin lips curled in disgust.

The pain throbbed on my arm, and I could feel the rage beneath the icy touch.

"Is that everything?" I asked, the questioning ending in a rasp,

"No," he replied shortly, his eyes still not leaving mine, making me feel like their darkness was slowly swallowing me. "I have unfinished business with that sister of hers as well."

"Ellie?"

His lips pulled back from his teeth at the sound of her name, and, for a second, I saw behind his veneer of composed refinement.

"Why not tell them yourself?" I asked, a little desperate. "Why waste your time with me?"

All at once, he seemed to gather himself. Drawing his rage back into whatever frigid abyss that lived inside him.

"Do you think that idea didn't occur to me? That I would have bothered finding you if there was a choice?" Cal asked, barely disguising his incredulity.

I shuddered, the oily grip on my arm tightening,

His voice was stiff as he continued,

"Unfortunately, to speak to them directly has been deemed... unacceptable. As a consequence, I am forced to use you to pass on my words."

For no more than a moment, Cal's face contorted, a physical expression of his intense irritation.

"But, I suppose it is fortunate you are a willing messenger." He added thoughtfully, as all traces of anger disappeared from his face, "as I am not so easily dissuaded from my desires."

I wanted to lean away, yet the vile, otherworldly grip on my increasingly numb arm didn't lessen, and my crippled fingers were still unresponsive when I tried to move them. Cal smiled, watching me flex my captured hand with little success. I wondered if he hoped I'd try to pull away to have an excuse to inflict more pain. Suddenly, David appeared in my mind in a blaze of light, his memory enough warmth for me to finally find that spark of courage again.

"I'm not a willing messenger." I snapped, fear and adrenaline shivering back to life in my frozen body, "and I'm not going to help you. The fact Athena May even wrote down your name is more than you deserve. If anyone should be forgotten, it's you!"

For a moment, the night seemed to inhale sharply, the shadows themselves taken by surprise. I stiffened, my shoulders hunching as I prepared for the expected onslaught of pain.

Instead, Cal laughed.

The sound was awful, humourless and mocking, turning my brave words into nothing.

"Oh Jenna, you are so much more amusing than I'd hoped and such an appealing temper, too." He smiled, and the oily hands sharply tugged me closer to his shadowy frame.

"I still require my message to be relayed, but now, as I look more closely, there's a far more pleasurable way you can be of use to me, "his voice sliding over my skin like oil, "a long-denied desire that I don't doubt you can, shall we say, alleviate?"

His gaze burned, leisurely running over my body with unashamed lust,

"And, be assured, despite what you might have been led to believe, I am not a selfish man, you would find yourself suitably... entertained."

Nausea rose in me, like a hand choking my neck. Images spun through my mind like a terrifying carousel of nightmares when I realised Cal's inhuman powers were matched only by the sheer depravity of his mind. His smile grew as he felt my panic; the frenetic pounding of my heart was unquestionably audible to us both.

"Although," he said, reaching out one long-fingered hand to barely graze my cheek, "I suspect there isn't enough time to fulfil all my deepest-held expectations, and I'd be left unsatisfied, which, to say the least, would be profoundly disappointing."

189

Cal dropped his hand, and the skin on my face felt raw.

"So, perhaps it is time for us to part, Jenna." He said, and I looked down to see the oily black mark on my arm slipping away into the shadows. I gritted my teeth at the rush of hot blood to my numb hand.

"Go, before I change my mind and decide to keep you, I freely admit to being intrigued to see just how long it would take for you to resist real temptation. You see, for all the fake veneer of morality, I saw it in your eyes, that darkness within you that is just waiting to be released."

I shuddered at the closeness of his voice and shook my head but felt deeply uncomfortable with the notion that maybe there was some degree of truth in his assertion. But before I could speak, Cal stepped back and waved a dismissive hand at me, "but for now, that will have to be a pleasure for another time."

I stumbled forward before there was a sudden grip on my neck, a burning cold that oozed around my throat, holding me still. I opened my mouth to scream, but there was no sound other than his voice, disembodied and spoken as if it came from every shadow around me.

"Oh, I nearly forgot- I do hope you like what I've done with the house. I've added something special which will add some much-needed warmth."

Feeling suddenly free, I spun around, yet no one was there. Only an odd darkness remained, an oil-stained outline of a man which glinted once, as if mockingly winking at me, before dissolving into nothing. The cold fear fading from my mind allowed my thoughts to flow, and in a moment of horrible clarity, I understood. Without pausing, I ran along the street, Cal's last words repeating in my mind, there was only one place he could have meant- Athena May's home. Raw horror gripped my chest as I stood on the kerbside and stared at the house, which had felt like my only haven until this moment. But now flames danced wildly, devouring the fabric of the building that held all those precious moments and filled with despair, and my heart plummeted. Firefighters swarmed the scene; their anxious yet forceful voices rang out as chaos reigned, all smothered by the acrid, black smoke that billowed into the sky, obscuring the once quiet neighbourhood. Panic surged through my veins, and dense air filled my straining lungs with a sense of impending loss.

I was frozen in disbelief, eyes darting from one officer to another, hoping to catch a glimpse of reassurance. But there was no time, their determined expressions betrayed the gravity of the overall situation, so could not be distracted by my need for comfort. Each passing moment felt like an eternity, my mind racing to comprehend the magnitude of the blaze.

All those treasured hours with Athena May were being savagely engulfed in the inferno's wrath, and I was powerless. The fragile walls that had silently witnessed all that maelstrom of emotions were now crumbling beneath the relentless assault of the flames. Fragments of my life and, more importantly, Athena May's, being reduced to ash and smoke, whispered their final goodbyes on the heat-filled wind.

Amidst the chaos, a lone firefighter approached, his eyes weary but resolute. He offered a reassuring nod, a silent promise that they would do everything in their power to save what could be salvaged. As he passed me, a young woman forcefully grabbed his arm.

"I'm from News Today. Was there anyone in there?" she barked. Her question suddenly made me realise that Athena May might have been inside when the blaze took hold.

"The crews are dealing with it; there'll be a press conference at some stage when we know more," he replied briskly before racing to answer the call from his colleague. The young woman shook her head with evident frustration before turning to me,

"I don't suppose you anything?" she asked doubtfully; when I shook my head, she spun on her heel and hurried down the street to question the small group of onlookers that had gathered.

Finally, after what seemed like an eternity, the flames began to relent. The house was now a blackened skeleton with only wisps of blue-black smoke rising like ghostly spirits from the charred remains. The last few firefighters emerged, their soot-streaked faces etched with exhaustion and a degree of relief that they had finally been able to tame the beast.

"Do you know how the fire started?" called a woman, leaning out of the window from a house on the opposite side of the street, clearly dressed in her nightgown. One of the firefighters looked up at her, answering that the investigation was ongoing, so it was too early to tell.

"Were there any dead bodies in there?" she asked, her eyes shining with excitement. This time, he chose not to answer and simply threw his gear into the back of the truck, which looked like it was done with more than a bit of disgust at her almost gleeful enquiry. Seeing she would learn nothing more, she slammed her window shut and disappeared into her own house.

When everyone had left, and the chaos subsided, I stood alone, having barely made any movement since I'd arrived on the scene. A few curious people stopped and stared at the ruined home but quickly went on their way. I considered slipping under the tape for a moment to see if anything could be saved. Still, aside from the possible risk of falling debris, it was clear there was little chance of anything having survived. So I just stood and stared, my mind a whirlwind of uncertainty. Where could I go now? Should I just turn and go home? But if I did, would Athena May come there? Where would I find her now that the house was gone? The weight of indecision settled upon my shoulders, sinking me into a sea of confusion. After several minutes, the park came to my mind. It was peaceful there; maybe I could think more clearly about what to do next. I pictured the carved bench by the lake. It had also become a special place, so after finally deciding on this plan, I turned away from the still-smouldering timbers and made my way there.

As I reached the park, all the chaotic destruction of the fire and the terrifying encounter with Cal began to slowly fade into the back of my mind. The dew-filled stillness of the early morning seemed to seep into my skin, cooling the tumultuous emotions that had consumed me. A chilled breeze rippled through the trees as if gently urging me forward to that weathered bench, where comfort was waiting for me. With each step, memories from the notebook flooded my mind, painting vivid pictures of all of Athena May's stories, each one filled with gained wisdom and long-held dreams.

Arriving at the lake's edge, I found the bench nestled amongst the trees, its intricate carvings a testament to the skill of its creator. I traced the patterns with my fingertips, feeling the etchings beneath my touch. The wood, worn and weathered, seemed to hold the collective memories of all who had sought something intangible there before me. Taking a seat, I closed my eyes and let the tranquillity of the scene wash over me. Even though my whole body felt relaxed, as if infused by the natural peace, my hands held tightly to my bag that contained the notebook. There was no way I would ever allow it to become lost again, especially now, after the terrible fire. As the sun steadily rose over the horizon, casting a warm glow upon the water, I could feel its warmth on my face, like a loving hand gently touching my cheeks. Suddenly, I became aware of a rustling sound. When I opened my eyes, a small, silver-grey squirrel was perched on a nearby tree branch, nibbling on a pearl-like seed. Its dexterous little paws turned and twisted around its prize while its bushy tail swayed to the rhythm of the breeze like a softly feathered banner. The squirrel seemed oblivious to me as I watched it jump effortlessly from branch to branch, exploring the tree's canopy with no apparent fear of falling. As it disappeared into the leaves, I couldn't help but wonder what it would be like to be quite so fearless. I closed my eyes again, and after only a few minutes, this time, it was a familiar voice that broke the silence,

"I was hoping you would come here, child."

I opened my eyes and was both surprised and relieved to see Athena May sitting next to me, the morning sun illuminating her presence with a pale golden glow.

"The house," I spluttered, "there was a fire, there was nothing I could do."

She nodded and calmly explained that she was aware of the incident, quickly adding that there was no need for me to feel, in any way, responsible. At first, I hesitated to voice my belief that Cal Mulvane had caused the fire, but then it felt wrong to keep anything from her, and so with faltering words, I told her about his visit. When I had finished, there was a pause as I waited expectantly for her to say something about him, but the calm tone of her voice showed no trace of anger.

"Like all things in nature, we all return to the earth to provide space and nutrition for new life. It was time for the house to go, over the years, it had unquestionably fulfilled its purpose, and now it can make way for another home. So his intention to cause harm has actually brought about the start of a period of rejuvenation that will, in time, bring something stronger and more lasting than what was there before."

I was dumbfounded by her calm acceptance of the loss and the news about Cal, so I repeated the part where he had suggested that this visit might be the first of many. Athena May sighed and shook her head,

"He can do nothing to you, child, and I say with total certainty he will not be able to come back. The amount of energy he used will not be replaced, and that dark soul is now helpless and truly lost for eternity."

Without giving me much time to respond, Athena May asked why I had been at the house.

"I'd read the part about your sister, Ellie," I began, awkwardly pulling the book from my bag, "after she came to my home and said to mention the name to you."

The old lady shifted slightly at the mention of his name,

"It seems my past is making a habit of visiting you, and I am sorry, child, especially for the unwelcome attention of Mr Mulvane."

"Oh, he isn't important," I replied quickly as if trying to convince myself more than her.

"It wasn't because of him I wanted to talk with you; it was one particular part in your journal," I continued, flicking through the pages until I found the right place, "where you made the vow to never let anyone fall again."

I offered her the book while contemplating how to ask if that was why she had shown such an interest in me. But when Athena May merely glimpsed and sighed heavily, I said nothing.

"It was an intensely painful time," she said quietly, "it's always in my heart, the crippling guilt and shame at what happened."

Feeling I had unintentionally poured salt onto an open wound, I immediately closed the book and struggled to find anything more to say, consciously ignoring the many questions that were bubbling in my mind, wanting to be asked. We sat in silence until, at last, Athena May placed her handbag at her feet and rested back slightly on the bench.

"I remember when she came into the world," she said quietly, "The birth of any child is perhaps the most miraculous event in all of creation. It is a moment of pure, unadulterated joy for all those around them as a new life enters the world, full of promise and potential. I will never forget the day Ellie was born. It was so hot, and every living thing seemed to be seeking shelter, from the birds in the trees to the bees that drifted lazily through the air rather than exert themselves by flying. My grandmother was tending to Mama while my father and I sat outside," She paused and looked at me, her face beaming, "I say sat, but my father was up and down like there were live animals in both his pockets!"

We both chuckled, and she continued with her story, "After what felt like days, at last, we heard a tiny cry, and my grandmother appeared at the front door. She looked exhausted; beads of sweat hung like pearls from her hair. But there was a smile that stretched from one side of her face to the other.

"You have a new daughter," she announced, the words had barely left her mouth when my father ran past her and into the house. A few minutes later, I went inside. The air was stifling hot, and there was a strong smell of some kind of antiseptic, which made my eyes slightly water. I quickly wiped my face before taking a few steps closer to my parent's bed, where my mother was resting.

"Say hello to your sister, her name is Elizabeth Rose." The old lady said the name with such obvious pride and affection that I had to swallow hard as it felt like I was on the verge of tears. Athena May turned to look at me, "You know, the first time I held that tiny newborn baby in my arms, the most overwhelming feeling of wonder and awe washed over me. I could hardly believe the softness of her skin, the sweet scent of her breath, and the way her eyelashes fluttered. Oh, and those eyes! So wide and yet filled with a kind of wisdom, like she had been born with so much knowledge inside that perfect little head."

"It must have been an amazing moment," I said quietly.

"Oh Jenna, for all the places I have been and all the extraordinary things I've seen, nothing has come anywhere near as beautiful as seeing Elizabeth Rose for the first time."

We sat in silence, as I could see she was reliving the moment, and then she explained that when her sister was born, she had just lost two front teeth. So she couldn't say the word 'Elizabeth', and so that's how this new addition to the family became known as 'Ellie.'

"I was there for everything," Athena May continued, "she became an endless source of fascination and joy as she started to discover the world. Her first steps, first words, and I was even there when we saw that first smile; it was like we had the sun itself inside the house when that little girl smiled."

"Did you always get on with each other?" I asked. Athena May looked at me with mock horror, placing her hand on her chest and theatrically gasping.

"Absolutely not!" she exclaimed, "We would fight over almost anything, but every night after we had bathed and were tucked up in bed, we would always say we were sorry...every time," she reached for her handkerchief and dabbed her eyes. I didn't want to upset her any further by asking more questions, so I shifted back and gazed out at the lake. Athena May shook her head slightly, and she exhaled as if this action would release the sadness that was trapped inside her body. I was about to ask if she was alright when another voice spoke from behind us.

"I can't believe you remember."

Athena May looked over her shoulder and audibly gasped, "Ellie!"

The old lady looked genuinely shocked for the first time since we met as her sister sauntered around from behind the bench and stood before us.

"You look old," she began, cocking her head to one side, "but then I guess a lot of time has passed."

"Way too much time. I looked for you everywhere I could imagine you might be, but I always arrived just too late," the old lady's voice quivering and cracking with emotion. "You have to believe I tried to find you."

The younger woman pouted and shrugged her shoulders, "Oh, I know you did, but I just didn't want to be found, so I kept moving. Mostly around the city, but I did go back home once."

Athena May appeared genuinely surprised by this statement, which held more meaning than the almost casual way Ellie had delivered the line.

"You did? I haven't been back for years. Has it changed at all?"

Again, Ellie shrugged her shoulders,

"I guess the land is the same, but the old house has gone, and they've changed the church near Grandma's house. Do you remember the old cross?" She paused and waited for her sister to acknowledge the question, "Well, they've replaced that with one that lights up."

Athena May shook her head,

"She would hate that, the house of the Lord is…"

"No place for neon," interrupted Ellie.

As the two sisters faced each other, I felt distinctly awkward; there was clearly a great deal for them to say, and none of it was any of my business. So I rose from the bench and walked down to the edge of the lake to give them some space to talk, resisting the urge to look back. At first, I heard raised voices, but after some considerable time, the tone had shifted from confrontational to one that sounded far more affectionate. Although I was too far away to distinguish specific words, there was no question the mood had shifted. The curiosity within me was growing, so I focused all my attention on a family of swans that were gracefully gliding across the serene water. Their feathers, a pristine white, shimmered in the gentle sunlight, their long necks arched in elegant unison, rhythmically gazing down at their fluffed babies that scurried to keep up with their parents. As I watched, there was a distinct presence next to me; just from the sweet scent, I knew it was Ellie.

"I have to go, so I wanted to say goodbye," she began falteringly, "you know, I came to you as a child as I wasn't sure of you, and it seemed that no half-decent person would be unkind to a little girl."

"And you're sure of me now?" I asked, keeping my eyes fixed on the swans.

"From everything Athena May has said, it's through talking to you she has been made to think again about everything," she paused, "so thank you for that," the last phrase spoken in a deeper and more hushed tone.

"Is everything alright now between you?" I asked, finally turning to look at Ellie, she smiled and nodded her head.

"We should have spoken so long ago, but she was too lost in her feelings and as for me. Well, I was way too stubborn. I wanted her to suffer, and that was wrong," she admitted, "but now everything is right again, so we can both finally move on."

Before I could reply, she glanced back at Athena May, "Don't be too long, okay?" she called, her face brimming with pure happiness, and then she instructed me to go and talk with her sister again.

"She still has things to share with you, so make sure you listen very carefully."

Before she could leave, I felt compelled to ask a question, but as it formed in my mind, it seemed stuck, as if it was refusing to be asked. Somehow, Ellie sensed my growing discomfort,

"You want to ask something, don't you?" she began, her eyes glowing with mischief, without giving me a chance to reply, she smiled before adding thoughtfully, "Let's just say I moved on a long time ago to a better place, but that doesn't stop me from wanting to visit every so often."

Still feeling bemused, I chose to simply nod my apparent understanding of her enigmatic answer and wished her well. Then I hurried back towards the bench where Athena May was waiting for me. Deep in my soul, I somehow knew this might be the last time I saw her, just from what Ellie had said. This sad reality was almost impossible to contemplate, as it meant trying to live without her wisdom and compassion. Her presence had changed everything; it had been my only connection to the world, and now I was faced with going back to being completely alone. Only when I sat beside her did I realise Ellie had gone, leaving the lake to the swans, their rippling reflections dancing beneath them.

"You have to go too, don't you?" I said, my voice little more than a whisper, acutely aware I was being selfish, I quickly added that I was relieved that there had been an opportunity to talk with Ellie.

Athena May smiled sadly,

"It took way too long," she said unknowingly, echoing the same sentiment as her sister, "but at last, we have found peace and rediscovered our love for each other. I am so thankful the time came to put the weight of it all down."

"I don't know how it will be without you," I said, the words spilling from my mouth before I'd had a chance to filter them or, at the very least, sound less childlike. The old lady sighed and turned to look at me,

"You know something, child, there have been many times when I have been anxious, especially when I have found myself standing at the edge of the unknown, staring out into the vast expanse of the future. The road ahead seemed shrouded in an impenetrable mist, a swirling, shifting mass of uncertainty that seemed to stretch out endlessly before me. Just like you are now, I felt small and vulnerable, like a tiny boat tossed about on a stormy sea. But I kept going, and I know you can too because it's the only way any of us will see what lies beyond the horizon."

I nodded my understanding and wanted to reply with something equally wise and profound, but if those thoughts were there at all, they failed to come to mind. Athena May rose slowly from the bench, pausing only to gather her handbag, and I stood before her, my heart saddened, knowing what was to come. The sun's rays bathed us both in pure light, tinged with shimmering gold, as I stood there, still wishing that I could find the right words. But how could I possibly sum up everything that had happened between us in a simple goodbye? But that didn't stop the weight of those unuttered emotions from pressing against my chest, threatening to suffocate the last few moments we had left.

Yet, precisely as she had said so often, amidst the pain, I felt profoundly grateful for everything we had shared and the love that had brought us together. Like stars in the night sky, those memories would forever illuminate the path ahead.

But as I tentatively reached out to touch her hand, suddenly, the old fear came back that Athena May was nothing more than a figment of my imagination. For a moment, I was sure I would feel nothing but perhaps a cool mist, but then, it was there. The unmistakable warmth of another person, as my fingertips grazed her outstretched palm, I felt her tightly grip my hand. Our eyes locked, and in that silent exchange, we understood that this moment didn't mark the end of anything. It was merely a fork in the road where we had to follow different paths.

"You know something, child? Accepting that some things cannot change is one of the hardest lessons I have learned in life. It took me a long time, but in the end, I realised that while we may not be able to control the world around us, we can control our reactions to it. We can choose to find the silver lining in any situation, to focus on the positive instead of dwelling on the negative. Do you see why I'm sharing this with you at this particular time?"

She looked at me with a rare intensity, her large eyes scanning my face, perhaps hoping to see some sign that I genuinely understood.

"I believe I do," I replied as truthfully as I could, "although that silver lining isn't especially easy to see right now."

Athena May whispered what might have been a prayer and then released her hold on me. The tears welled in my eyes, cascading down my cheeks like a gentle rain, as I watched her slowly walk away, her head held high, looking stately, almost majestic, but without a backward glance. I waited, hoping she might stop and turn to wave, but I somehow knew it wasn't going to happen. So, instead, I craned to not lose sight of her as she disappeared into the distance.

For several minutes, I stood there, unable to move, as the echoes of our connection reverberated through my being. Not knowing why, I looked back down at the bench and almost cried out with overwhelming relief to see the edge of the notebook peeking out from the top of my bag. There was still more to read, and as I gathered up my belongings, I found myself wondering perhaps that was why Athena May hadn't looked back, as she had known, in some way, this wasn't a goodbye at all.

CHAPTER ELEVEN

When I arrived home, the air was heavy with an almost eerie stillness, and there was pure silence. The noise of the traffic outside barely registered, and there was no sound of people talking and laughing as they passed by the house. The house had always been quiet, but now it felt like a hollow shell, which was deeply unnerving. As I walked along the hallway, the vacant rooms stared back at me, almost as if they were mildly surprised to see any sign of life at all.

As I hurried along the hallway, every creaking floorboard beneath my feet groaned. The emptiness started to seep into my bones, and the same thought reverberated around my mind: had it always been this way? Had I just been so lost in my mind that I hadn't noticed? I glanced through an open doorway and saw furniture, once arranged with care by my mother, sat untouched and forlorn. The faded cushions sagged while the few rays of sunlight that managed to filter through half-closed blinds cast a melancholic glow upon the deserted rooms.

The absence of any aroma in my abandoned kitchen hung heavy in the air. During the worst times, there had always been some signs of the space being used, even if it was no more than a few scattered breadcrumbs or the heady scent of coffee. But now, the countertops were barren but for a thin layer of undisturbed dust. The only discernible sound of any kind of life was the soft hum of the refrigerator that stood alone as if awake while everything around it was in a deep, untroubled sleep.

I half-ran upstairs and went straight into my bedroom, unlike the rest of the house, it felt warm and almost welcoming. I kicked off my shoes and slid under the covers, relieved to feel the familiar cosiness of the soft blankets. After rearranging my pillows, I heaved my bag onto my lap and pulled out the notebook. Walking through the house had been undeniably troubling, to say the least, but I reasoned it could be fixed. In the morning, I could go back down and open the windows, maybe even deep clean every room. That would undoubtedly lift the overwhelming gloom and make the whole place feel more alive again. With this decision, I tossed the bag onto the floor and opened the book.

Many years ago, a life-changing event happened that began with me thinking I was simply going to see a brand new play, and so even though I'm guilty of thinking I've seen everything, I knew there were new voices to be heard,

*and I could not wait to listen to them. As I took my seat,
there was a heady mixture of anticipation, hope and
curiosity. And then, when I started to wonder if it would
ever begin, the red velvet curtains parted, unveiling a
world ready to share its untold story.*

*Within moments of appearing on the stage, the actors
began to weave their magic, creating an entire tapestry of
emotions that unfolded before my eyes. Every word was like
poetry, as they spoke of love and loss, of triumph and
despair, effortlessly bridging the vast chasm between
reality and imagination. Oh, and the set design! Simply a
work of art! The sheer scale and intricacy transported the
audience to a distant land in a different era. I could hardly
believe the attention to detail and all the extraordinary
craftsmanship that brought this world to life.*

*As then, as the performance reached its climax, I felt the
power of the story almost coursing through my veins. More
than once, I found myself fighting the urge to stand up and
wildly applaud, whereas other scenes were so
heartbreaking it was all I could do not to openly weep. The
play had become a journey, and I, along with the rest of the
audience, had become willing travellers, enchanted and
transformed. Eager to follow where we were being led
without even the slightest hesitation.*

And as we left the theatre, it felt like my heart was ablaze,
and it was clear everyone else felt much the same way.
Walking along the street, we all talked incessantly about
every aspect of the story: the performances, the music and
the impossibly beautiful ending. We had entered the theatre
as total strangers, and yet now, only a matter of hours
later, we had shared something so phenomenal the memory
would bind us together forever.

But there was so much more to spring from that already
memorable evening. In many ways, it was a day like any
other when the universe conspired to bring forth a
connection that would weave its way into the very core of
my life. Because after the play, amid the bustling crowd,
our paths converged. I found myself talking with this most
extraordinary man, his presence commanded my attention,
drawing me towards him like a moth to a flame. There was
an undeniable aura of strength and vulnerability that
radiated from him, a magnetic pull that defied explanation.
Our eyes met, and in that instant, time ceased to exist. It
was as if the universe had pressed pause, allowing us to
savour the weight of that shared gaze, the unspoken
understanding that passed between us. I have to confess,
until that moment, there had been many times when I'd
dismissed the notion of love at first sight as something that

only happened within the lines of a novel. But I was being proved wrong!

We talked with complete ease; every sentence he spoke unravelled another layer of his personality, revealing a depth of character that resonated with me on a deeply personal level. Being with him, I felt seen, heard, and understood in a way I had never experienced before. We arranged to meet again the next evening, and throughout the whole of the following day, I was like an excited schoolgirl. I had been on many dates before and had enjoyed time with lovers, all of whom had brought something unique to my life, although not all in a positive way. But I knew this was different, and it filled me with a level of anxious anticipation which was almost entirely new for me while being affectionately entertaining for my coworkers.

During that second evening, our connection deepened; it felt as if we had known each other long before we had actually met. Our shared laughter echoed through the chambers of my heart, creating a symphony of joy that reverberated through my very bones. Over the weeks that followed, in his arms, I grew to find comfort and a quiet strength that made me feel safe when life became too much. His touch ignited a fire within me, a passion that burned brightly. I discovered a love that was both tender and fierce, that I knew could weather any storm and joyously revel in every triumph.

Looking back, it was at that moment, walking away from the theatre, that on some level, I knew I had found the man who would become my husband. Our hearts had collided, and from that day forward, our journey would be a testament to the power of love and the beauty of two souls finding their homes in each other. After a year of marriage, within the depths of my soul, a truth unfolded like a delicate blossom, its petals unfurling slowly, revealing a profound reality that would shape the contours of our life together. It bore the weight of unshed tears and silent longing when I finally realised, with a heavy heart, that the gift of motherhood was not destined to grace my path.

Like the bittersweet notes of a mournful melody, this revelation echoed through the chambers of my heart. All the dreams we had shared of cradling a new life were now but wistful wisps of a cherished fantasy. Robert and I had to accept that the joyous laughter, the endless enquiring minds and the sheer wonder of our children would never be within our reach. After our worst fears had been confirmed, for many months, when I was alone, I wept at what felt like a cruel injustice, and I know my beloved husband undoubtedly did the same.

But then, as time passed and with the help of those closest to us, we started to see that maybe there was a way to redefine the meaning of parenthood. So, we made the conscious decision that even though we could not have our own children, perhaps we could offer our love and compassion in another way and embrace those who needed support and guidance. So, this became a part of our lives, and together, we helped with a variety of youth organisations and found our place within the lives of many; even when it could only be temporary, there was a joyful satisfaction in feeling we were making a positive impact. We poured our love into the lives of others, offering warm acceptance and providing unwavering support.

It was at this time I slowly nurtured the fragile blossoms of creativity by sowing seeds of inspiration that would flourish and bloom in the fertile soil of possibility. I began to write, hoping to share my love of the written word with every young person I encountered and as can happen, what started as a trickling stream of work became a cascading waterfall. Many nights, I would sit at my desk and create worlds, all of which Robert visited, offering his kind criticism that was always tempered by his unfailing

encouragement and undeniable pride in me. When we saw
my first publication in a shop window, neither of us moved
for several minutes, glancing from the display to each other
with wide-eyed wonder. I thought back to that little girl
who only owned one book, how amazed would she be? That
many years later, her own words would be captured within
a similarly thin volume for the whole world to read. We
dined out that evening at a restaurant that was probably
well beyond our financial means, but my darling husband
insisted on marking the occasion. He raised his glass to me,
adding there was no question; this would be the first of
many books- as, in so many ways, he was proved to be
correct.

I was to be married to my beloved Robert for over twenty-
five years before that beautiful heart he had carried in his
chest finally could not support him any longer. The grief I
felt when he passed was intensely painful as, for the longest
time, it was like I had lost a physical part of my own body.
But now, so many years later, I can see how blessed I was
to have shared my life with such a person.

One final thought before I close this journal and retreat to
my bed: I don't believe it is a coincidence that I chose
today to write about looking back and what might lie ahead
in the future. As if there was any risk of my becoming stale

or disinterested in life, my visit to the theatre served to
remind me that there is still so much more to come. As
someone once said, who is far wiser than me, we all know
what we already know, the real joy in life is discovering
those things we don't know yet.

I read and re-read that last sentence with such focus it was
like I was trying to burn those words into my memory so it
would be impossible to forget them. I didn't feel as if I
knew very much at all, but perhaps I was wrong. I put the
notebook on my bedside table and decided to try and sleep
for a while, as it felt after all the emotions of the day, it
would be wise just to rest, especially since I had so much to
do in the morning. I chose to only take half my usual
medication as it should be enough to bring some peace.

The next day, without allowing myself time to think, I
began to bring life back into the house. I pulled back the
curtains and flung open the windows, and almost
immediately, it felt as if the building sighed with
unrestrained pleasure. Sunlight poured through the dusty
windows, casting a warm, amber glow onto the long-
neglected wooden floors. It had been months since I had
felt the energy to rise from the depths of my despair, but
something within me had stirred, an ember of
determination that whispered, "It's time."

With each step, I felt the weight of my past clinging to my weary limbs. The deep scars of the battle with my all-consuming depression had bled into the very fabric of this house, a haunting reminder of the darkness. But today, it felt as if I had finally found the strength to take control of the mess that had mirrored the intense confusion within my mind. I gingerly picked up a cloth, and as I swept it across the dusty shelves, particles danced in the sunlight, a delicate ballet of neglect and renewal. It felt as if those specks carried fragments of memories, all that time I had spent buried in sorrow, too lost to notice the world around me. So they had to be freed, to be allowed to dissipate into the wider atmosphere and not be bound to me any longer. With every movement, I could feel the layers of desolation lifting, replaced by a glimmer of hope. It was as if dusting away the cobwebs, I was unravelling the web of desperation that had held me prisoner for far too long. In a concerted effort to maintain momentum, I switched on the radio, and joyful music filled the air, glorious guitar riffs with soaring vocals echoed through the house, bringing life back to what had been near-dead spaces.

The vacuum, humming softly, devoured the debris with a voracious hunger as if driven to rid my home of the negative energy. Even though I was well aware it was only symbolic with each swipe of the sponge, I forced myself to believe that I was removing the stains of self-doubt and self-loathing. The heady aroma of lemon-scented cleaner filled the air, mingling with the scent of my newly discovered purpose. Hours turned into moments as I tirelessly scrubbed, rearranged, and reimagined the space that had become a battleground. While I transformed the house, each cluttered room soon exuded a kind of calm that had been absent for as long as I could remember.

When I had finally finished, I felt utterly exhausted, but as I stood in the doorway, a surge of gratitude swelled within me. I knew there was so much more to this morning than simply creating a tidy home, it was also the first step to reclaiming myself. This act of cleaning would seem mundane to anyone else, but had been an act of defiance against the darkness that had almost swallowed me. I knew the war wasn't over, but it felt like, finally, I had won a battle. After a long, hot shower, I settled onto my bed and, for a moment, just breathed in the flowery fragrance of my clean sheets. Reluctantly, I listened to the voicemails from my therapist and called her office, making an appointment for the end of the week. I had no idea how I was going to even begin to explain everything to her, as I could barely make any real sense of it all myself. I glanced down at the notebook, with every fibre of my being, I wanted to settle down and read more. However, after glimpsing into the refrigerator that was bereft of food, I knew I had to buy some groceries. At first, I hesitated, the prospect of actually walking amongst a crowd of people again made me feel distinctly anxious. But, after several attempts at walking through the front door, I finally lost patience with myself and went out into the street.

When I arrived at the shopping mall, the fluorescent lights flickered above me, casting a bright and sterile glow onto the neatly arranged aisles. It had been months since I last stepped foot into this place, and, at first, it felt as if the quickened rhythm of my heartbeat was echoing in my ears. So, I consciously focused on the chatter of the other shoppers and the distant melodies drifting from unseen speakers. Rather than give into the desire to race around the store, I made myself walk slowly and actually look at the displays rather than stare down at the floor, which had been my usual practice in the past. When I reached the fresh produce section, I reached out, my fingers grazing the smooth surface of a ripe peach. Its scent wafted towards me, and with a remembered appreciation, I carefully selected a few pieces of fruit, cradling them in my hands as if they were precious gems.

Moving through the store, I discovered aisles filled with ingredients and spices from all over the world, and my mind instantly recalled Athena May talking about her travels. I felt a wave of nostalgia but refused to allow myself to become lost in its melancholy and instead simply smiled at the memory. When I reached the checkout, the cashier smiled warmly when I greeted her, and we exchanged pleasantries while packing my shopping. For her, it must have been just an everyday moment in her day, but for me, it was almost unbelievable to think this was even possible.

Leaving the store, I stepped out into the sunlight, the weight of my shopping bags a comforting reminder of every step I had taken during the day. As I carried them home, I could feel my body beginning to struggle, but it was a good kind of weariness. After making myself lunch, I sat down on the sofa with Athena May's journal. For all the enthusiasm and positivity, I had managed to put into the day, I knew it was only one. If I were to make these feelings last, I needed to hear her voice, as it would be too easy to slip back into the darkness that I knew was waiting for me to fall.

As I grew older, life became more and more of a journey. There were moments of joy and wonder but also times of heartache and disappointment. Through it all, I learned that this was the definition of having a full life, a succession of ups and downs, twists and turns. But no matter what obstacles I faced, thanks to my upbringing, I always found a way to persevere and keep moving forward.

The next morning, I woke up early and felt the urge to witness the sunrise. I slipped on my shoes and headed out to the nearby park. As I walked through the quiet streets, I couldn't help but feel a sense of anticipation. The world was still asleep, and I was alone with my thoughts once again.

As I approached the park, I could see the sky beginning to lighten. The first hints of pink and orange were just starting to appear on the horizon. I found a quiet spot by the lake and sat down on a carved wooden bench, waiting for the sun to rise. The air was cool and crisp; the only sounds were a lone bird heralding the new day with its song and the faint rustling of the leaves overhead. As the sun began to creep over the horizon, a warm glow filled the sky. The colours were breathtaking - a riot of pinks, oranges, and yellows that gradually brought light to every surface still shrouded in the blue mist of the morning. My original idea had been to only stay long enough to see the sunrise, but I was so content to be surrounded by the natural peace that I found no genuine desire to move.

As the sun rose higher in the sky, I noticed an older woman walking towards me. She had a kindly face with a warm smile; despite her age, she carried herself ramrod straight, and her steps were so light they barely seemed to touch the wet grass beneath her feet.

"Good morning," she said as she approached. "Beautiful day, isn't it?"

I smiled back and nodded, and we began to talk. I found myself drawn to her as she told me stories of her own life with all its joys and struggles while sharing some of the lessons she had learned along the way. She listened intently to my own, and the time flew by as our unhurried conversation continued. After almost an hour, we both realised that we should perhaps get moving, and as I rose from the bench, she offered me one piece of advice which I've kept close to my heart for all these years.

"Remember to always follow your heart," she said. "There will be times when the world seems to be pulling you in a hundred different directions. But if you listen closely, you'll always know which way to go."

As the older woman walked away, I took a deep breath and looked around me. The sun was now high in the sky, and the world was coming to life. Birds chirped in the trees, and the sound of traffic could be heard in the distance. Still feeling the benefit of the wonderful start to my day, later that same afternoon, I decided to host an informal dinner party for some close friends. I put on some music and started to prepare the food, feeling grateful for the opportunity to share some good company and conversation. As the evening wore on, I noticed that one of my friends, Catherine, seemed troubled. She was quiet and withdrawn, and her eyes seemed to hold a deep sadness. Finally, I took her aside and asked if she was okay. At first, she tried to brush it off, but eventually, she opened up and told me about some medical tests she had done. Although the doctors had assured her there was no reason to be fearful, the results were preying on her mind. I listened carefully and assured her I would be there for her, whatever the outcome. When she insisted there was no need for me to worry, I simply hugged her tightly and repeated my promise before reminding her of all the things she had done for me. As the night wore on, the mood at the party began to shift; even though our conversation had been entirely private, the other guests became more honest and open, and, in the end, we all shared stories of our struggles and triumphs. And as we said our goodbyes at the end of the night, Catherine thanked me again and said she felt less alone now. This was perhaps the best moment of the whole evening, and I was so happy I had been able to help such a good friend-even in such a small way.

As I lay in bed that night, I found myself thinking about the following day and the possibilities it held. There was a sense of anticipation building within me, a feeling that something new and exciting was about to begin. And as I drifted off to sleep, I knew what it was - I would try writing a book. Since I'd been a little girl, it had been a dream of mine to write my own story, having spent so much time enjoying the worlds created by others. For too long, I had been putting it off, telling myself that I didn't have the time or the energy to commit to such a big project. But now, with the lessons of the day fresh in my mind, I knew that it was a sign that I should leap - to follow my heart and pursue the creative passion that had been calling to me for so long.

The following day, I woke up early and sat down at my desk. I took a deep breath, opened a fresh notebook, and began to write. The words flowed easily like a river finding its course. As the days turned into weeks, the story took shape, filled with moments from my life, the good and the bad times, but all told in what I hoped would be easy for anyone else to read. And as I finished the final pages, I knew that this was more than just a book - it was a testament to everything I had ever learned but, more importantly, a loving tribute to everyone who had played a role in my life.

For in the end, it was the journey that had mattered - the lessons learned, the connections made, and the joy and beauty that had been woven into every moment along the way. As I wrote the last words, I prayed that perhaps one day, someone would read it and maybe find inspiration within the pages.

As the last few words registered in my mind, I felt the all too familiar grip of panic and flipped over the page, then the next, only to find they were empty. I had reached the end. I felt strangely abandoned, which made little or no sense as it was just a book, after all. After closing all the windows, I started to walk slowly upstairs. I felt a heaviness in my limbs, and even though I was aware of just how much better everywhere looked, it started to feel dull and lifeless again.

"Don't do this to yourself, Jenna," I said aloud, "Don't forget, there's the therapy appointment."

I clambered into bed and rested the journal on my chest, "I can read it all again," I reassured myself, "so there's no need to slip back."

I sighed heavily and switched off the light, it had been a good day; that was the important thing. Also, I still had the book, so nothing had been lost. I took the other half of my medication, slipped further under the covers and quickly fell asleep. But after only a few fitful hours, I was wide awake again, feeling as if my fragile positivity had evaporated entirely. Despite all my tossing and turning, I hadn't let go of Athena May's journal. I sat up and turned to the last page again, re-reading the line about not being alone.

"But I am," I said softly, "how am I going to keep going without you?"

I took another tablet and waited to sink into the drowsiness which thankfully came and made it impossible even for my troubled mind to hold onto even the most basic thought. When I awoke the next morning, my head felt heavy, and it took a few minutes before my eyelids found the motivation to open. At last, I found I could focus again and immediately realised the journal was resting open on the bed next to me. I rolled over to look more closely and read the exposed passage with a mix of absolute disbelief and complete relief.

Let me finish at the beginning....
Every evening of my life, wherever I might be, I spend a moment simply gazing at the horizon. As the sun sets ablaze, casting hues of gold and crimson across the vast expanse of sky. It is then I know, with total certainty, I am never alone. As I can feel the gentle touch of the evening air as the night breezes whisper through my hair. If I wait, I can see the stars sprinkled across the night sky, each one a twinkling light. Watching their glorious dance reminds me that light and hope surround me even in the darkest of nights.
If I listen carefully, I can hear the echoes of laughter and deep conversations drift through the air, reminding me of all the others who are sharing this same journey. But also, those who have gone before, who have left their footsteps for me to follow, showing me the right path. I am carried by their love and support, knowing that their presence guides me through the often-confusing maze of life.
So, don't look down, child, instead, make sure you keep your eyes fixed on the horizon. With each new day, I want you to try and embrace the unknown, knowing that you will

always be surrounded by those who love you and are
walking beside you, even when you believe you're alone. If
you can do this, I know you will find the strength to not
only continue, but also, you'll be able to embrace the
beauty of this remarkable journey.

Even though I struggled to read the last words as tears were
free-falling down my cheeks, I felt the weight of their
meaning in my heart. In the half-light, I could see the
picture of David and remembered his unadulterated love of
life. I had believed he had taken me with him when he had
died, but that has been so misguided. If I had really loved
him, I would be doing everything that he would have done,
and without really thinking, I heard myself apologising to
him for wasting so much time. As the last words slipped
from my mouth, my mind inexplicably turned to my
mother, and the weight of a thousand memories settled on
my shoulders. Without allowing myself time to change my
mind, I sat up, switched on the lamp and pulled out a sheet
of paper and a pen from my bedside table. Even though this
unexpected idea seemed vaguely ridiculous if I was being
logical, there was no way of ignoring the overwhelming
emotion that needed to be fulfilled. Writing anything
seemed impossible for a moment as my hand was

trembling, but after taking a few deep breaths, I began to write to my mother. For so long, the house had echoed with all the unspoken words, the heavy silence weighed down by regrets and missed opportunities, so following Athena May's example, this seemed like the way to finally give them all a voice.

As I began, the memories flooded forth like an unstoppable tide. I recalled the days when her vivacious presence had often filled our home. But then, as the years wore on, after my father had left us, how that laughter had turned to tears, and her joy gave way to a relentless battle against the demons that haunted her soul. Despite the stinging tears, I travelled back in time to revisit the moments when her addiction held our family captive. All the sleepless nights, the shattered promises, and the desperate pleas for her to choose a different path which, however loudly I spoke, somehow, she never heard. But I knew this letter shouldn't only be about dwelling on the pain but instead finding a place of forgiveness- not just for her but for myself. I poured my heart onto the paper, openly confessing my struggles and acknowledging my imperfections. I told her that, unlike when I was a child, I now understood addiction is a disease that can shackle even the strongest of souls and that she had been a victim of its relentless grip.

I wanted to show her I understood, expressing my heartfelt wish that there should have been more time for me to show her compassion when she was still alive instead of being distant and filled with deep-seated resentment. I wrote about my profound gratitude for providing for my future as it was clear my father had such interest and may well have left me homeless, but for her foresight. While writing the last few sentences, I started to feel the weight lift from my weary shoulders, even though my letter couldn't reach her. I still believed that perhaps, in some unknown way, she could feel what I had written.

When it felt as if there was nothing left to say, I carefully signed my name, and as I sealed the envelope, I spoke aloud to my mother. I asked her to forgive me for all the years I had blamed her for how my life had been. For a few moments, I waited, just in case there was some slight sound of a response, but even when none came, my heart still felt lighter. After carefully putting the letter in the drawer of my bedside table and checking if the journal was safe, I switched off the light. I settled under the covers, hoping against hope that one day, this newly found peace of mind might become permanent.

CHAPTER TWELVE

I awoke early the next morning, and before anything within my mind could make it impossible for me to move, I was up and dressed. As I made some breakfast, I put the TV on, as although the house felt infinitely warmer and more like a proper home, the silence was still hard to bear. As the screen leapt into life, the two overly perky presenters were beaming from behind their almost neon yellow desk. I sat down at the kitchen counter to watch and idly wondered how anyone could be that cheerful so early in the morning. The scripted banter flew between them, punctuated by dazzling smiles, and I couldn't help but speculate if they really liked each other at all. But then, their faces changed with a slightly overdone seriousness, which signalled the delivery of the following story required a degree of gravitas.

"And now over to our reporter, Claire Kelly, who has been at the press conference held by officials from the fire department regarding the recent blaze at the home of esteemed author Athena May Bower."

I froze as if I'd just been struck by lightning.

"The conference has just ended, and it seems the fire's source was faulty electrical writing in the kitchen. The house has been empty for some months since the author moved into the 'Silver Oaks' residential care facility, so the police are assuming perhaps a homeless person seeking shelter broke into the home."

The studio-based presenter continued with his face furrowed in an almost theatrical intensity.

"Do we know whether Athena May has been informed of the tragedy? It will be a terrible shock for such a frail old lady."

"She has been visited by victim support officers who reported that she is aware of what has happened but owing to her poor health. It's almost impossible to determine whether or not she fully grasps that her beloved home has gone."

Still wearing what had been deemed just the 'right' level of solemnity, the male presenter thanked his colleague, and the screen flickered back to the studio. As the couple instantly switched from their serious expressions to banter again, I switched off the TV. My mind was a total blur. Nothing made any sense; my thoughts simultaneously hurried down multiple paths of explanation, but they all led nowhere. I found myself pacing around the room, asking my questions aloud with only the silent walls acting as a patient audience. Finally, when I could almost feel my mind was heading to the edge of almost total madness, an idea managed to make its way through the mental chaos. I had to go to 'Silver Oaks.'

It took no more than a few moments to search for the place. My usual reluctance to go anywhere was easily overwhelmed by the all-consuming desire to find some answers. Less than an hour later, I had reached the wide-open gates of the facility, like two freshly painted arms welcoming anyone who cared to visit. As I took my first few hesitant steps, the landscape surrounding the main buildings unfolded before my eyes like an impressionist painting, each deft stroke imbued with a sense of slightly blurred beauty. The grounds were vibrant with life and colour, separated only by a meandering path lined with weathered stones and neatly clipped shrubs. The glorious flowers bowed and dipped their heads as I passed, as if welcoming my arrival with respectful reverence. Their delicate petals quivered with nervous anticipation.

Tall trees, their branches outstretched like gnarled fingers, stood along the perimeter of the gardens. Their leaves, bathed in shades of lush green and gold, rustled with gentle sighs.

In front of the largest building, a pond surrounded by elegant reeds reflected the vibrant palette of the sky. Ducks glided across the water, their movements slow and deliberate, as if mirroring the unhurried pace of life within these walls. The ripples they created expanded outward, like echoes, dissipating into the peaceful stillness of the air. Beyond the pond, an elegant gazebo stood as a solitary figure, slightly weathered by the elements. Its wooden beams and carved lattices creaked as if reminiscing together about everything that had happened under the ornate roof. I could see two people sitting inside, flanked by two others dressed in white uniforms. I could just hear them all laughing, the sound of their shared pleasure being carried on the wind.

As I walked into the hallway, a mix of emotions started to swirl, none of which stayed still long enough for me to identify them. After a brief conversation with a receptionist, which was primarily focused on her ensuring that I wasn't a journalist looking for a story. She permitted me to visit with Athena May after I had convinced her of our friendship. The scent of antiseptic hung heavy in the air, mingling with the faint aroma of roses. As I passed open doors, the rooms were brightly painted, and although some were occupied by a solitary figure, others had small groups involved in a variety of activities. The atmosphere was not one of ageing or any kind of sadness; it was more of a contented peace. I took comfort in the fact that if this was where Athena May was living, then it would certainly suit her. My heart, still fluttering with anticipation, led me to the room where I hoped to find my dear friend. We had shared so much, but now, standing outside her door, I couldn't help but wonder how much of those precious moments remained etched in her allegedly fragile mind. With a deep breath, I pushed open the door, revealing a room adorned with photographs and neat shelves lined with books. The golden sunlight streamed through a pair of half-open glass doors that led out into the gardens. Bathed in the soft glow, there was Athena May, sitting upright in a large, passed armchair, her hair glistening with thin strands of pure silver that shimmered like a halo. Her large eyes, once vibrant and full of mischief, now seemed vague, as if they were peering through a veil of forgotten years.

"Miss Athena May?" My voice trembled as if afraid to disturb the delicate existence that enveloped her. She turned her gaze towards me, and for a moment, something flickered in her eyes like a fleeting spark. But as quickly as it appeared, it seemed to vanish, leaving behind a void that pained my soul.

She smiled. "Hello, child, you must forgive me, but may I ask, have we met before? My memory is not always reliable."

I swallowed the lump that had formed in my throat, my heart ached as I acknowledged this reality. How could everything we had shared have slipped through the cracks of her mind? How was I going to find any answers from someone to whom I was nothing more than a stranger? But even though, for a brief moment, I wanted to make some excuse about coming to the wrong room. However difficult this might be, I owed it to her to stay. With trembling fingers, I reached out and took her frail hand in mine.

"It's me, Miss Athena May, Jenna, Jenna Howard."

On hearing my name, a definite glimmer of recognition danced in her eyes once more, and a slight smile tugged at the corners of her lips.

"Oh, my dear child, of course, yes, I remember now. How foolish of me to forget. Time has a way of playing tricks on us, doesn't it?"

Tears welled in my eyes as I nodded, my heart leapt with joy at seeing that wonderful face while feeling the profound connection we had shared. Despite everything, in this moment, nothing else mattered other than knowing the essence of our friendship still lingered as a fragile thread that refused to be severed.

As the hours passed, we sat side by side. I listened as she reminisced about her life, and although many of the stories were familiar to me, it was incredibly moving just to be in her presence again. She would pause and sip some water every so often, but her ability to weave a story remained undiminished by time or her failing memory. At last, when we were sitting in a comfortable silence, I tentatively raised the subject of the notebook. I pulled it from my bag and rested it on her lap. Her eyes filled with tears almost immediately as she lovingly stroked the cover.

"I cannot believe you kept this," she croaked, "when I heard about the fire, I was sure it was lost."

"No, I kept my promise to you to keep it safe, but perhaps now, I should return it to you."

She turned to me and slowly shook her head,

"No, child, I'd like you to have it, there are enough of my books out in the world. I believe this one is meant for you."

I thanked her and took it back, she smiled again while resting her head back on the chair. She looked weary and asked if I might help her get more comfortable. I did not want to hurt her, so I suggested calling a nurse to help her to bed, but Athena May assured me that we could manage together when the time was right. So, instead, I carefully pulled a soft blanket over her knees and then settled back.

"I really should let you rest," I said quietly, but her hand gripped mine with such unexpected force before I could even move.

"Wait with me, child," she replied, her voice now no more than a hushed whisper. Obediently, I followed her gaze, and we sat watching the sun slip silently down behind the trees.

"Don't forget, keep your eyes on the horizon," she added. Suddenly feeling as if she was slipping away from not only me but life itself, I clasped her hand and knew I had to ask one question, even though I was well aware it was selfish and whatever the answer might be, wouldn't change anything.

"How did you come to me? In the old house, how could you be there?"

Athena May smiled, almost as if she had been waiting for me to ask. She took a deep breath and then turned to look directly at me.

"I have lived a long time, child, and apart from all the things I have learned over the years. The most important lesson was understanding that a spirit, when it can be truly free, can transcend any limitation, cross every boundary of time and space."

She paused and took a deep breath. I could hear that she was struggling, but when I again attempted to insist, she rest, the old lady waved away my concern. Her expression was one of pure determination, as if, at that moment, there was nothing more important than what she had to say to me.

"You remember me telling you about my grandmother?" When I nodded, she took another breath.

"She was born into a world that sought to confine her, to mould her into something that those around her had decided was appropriate. But her spirit was like a flame that refused to be dimmed, so through every trial she faced, that great lady would overcome it with a strength that very often defied reason."

Athena May's face glowed with pride, her eyes sparkling defiantly in the face of the creeping exhaustion that was starting to affect her body.

"It was she who taught me that the human spirit is not bound by the confines of the body nor limited by the circumstances that surround it. It is a force that can embrace all the infinite possibilities that seem to lie beyond our grasp. Child, I cannot even begin to explain everything that happened when I was with her other than to say I saw dreams that defied all logic come true."

Once more, Athena May's body struggled to maintain pace with her words as she took another breath and sipped some water.

"When she died, I mourned her loss for some time. It was almost impossible to accept that she had gone and her light had been extinguished. But then, she appeared to me, as real as you and I are as we sit here together. At first, I was sure it was nothing more than my wishful thinking, but then, she spoke to me."

"What did she say?" I asked quietly. Athena May looked away from me and frowned slightly as, for a moment, she gazed wistfully out of the window. After a few moments of silence, I started to feel concerned, but before I could speak, the old lady recited her grandmother's words.

"Never forget that the human spirit can transform the mundane into the extraordinary, the ordinary into the sublime. It can rewrite everything that tries to contain us and reveal a limitless potential that is way beyond our understanding."

A smile of satisfaction spread across her face before she turned back to me.

"That night, I was visiting the house when you arrived, child, you were soaked through, and I could see you had reached the point of wanting to end your life." The words caught in her throat, and I could feel tears starting to trickle unchecked down my face.

"I couldn't leave you," she continued softly, "at least not until I was sure you wouldn't fall," she stopped again and looked at me with that familiar intensity.

"So, will you fall, child?"

I shook my head, now completely unable to speak and could only watch as she sighed with a rich contentment that seemed to radiate from the depths of her being. Athena May rested her head back and closed her eyes. I held her hand but not tightly as if somehow knowing it was time to let her go.

Leaving her was almost impossible, but when the nurses ushered me out of her room, I was left with no choice. But as I walked back down the path, there was no doubt in my mind that a piece of my heart would always be with her. From 'Silver Oaks', I went straight to the largest bookshop, remembering the news report had described Athena May as an author. As I walked along the bustling street, it seemed almost wrong that I didn't feel more distraught because she had died. But somehow, on some level, it didn't feel final.

More than once, I had witnessed the sheer power of her spirit, so to cry about her passing would have almost felt like a kind of betrayal, as if after everything she had shared with me, it would show I hadn't really listened at all. There was an undeniable sense of loss, a stubborn, dull ache in my chest, but the fact there might still be a way to hear more of her words kept pushing me forward, and I knew that was what she would want. After scouring through the stands, just when I considered leaving, suddenly, her name seemed to blaze out at me from the shelves.

At last, amongst a row of distinguished books, I found five volumes and, without pause, eagerly took them all. On reaching the checkout, I was met by a bored-looking assistant, who, on registering my presence, allowed his expression to shift into one of forced affability. He scanned each one with no more than a flicker of interest crossing his features as he registered the title and the author while explaining that I had been fortunate to get them. It seemed since the news story about the fire, there has been renewed interest in Athena May Bowers' work.

"It's almost vulgar how people want to own all of her books, purely based on a tragedy."

He sniffed, "I've had customers coming in all day, but they don't just want these," he added, packing my bag, "They're also looking for her journal. Absolutely ridiculous what people will believe these days."

"Journal?" I asked, hoping I sounded suitably casual.

"Some of her new *fans,*" he said with a sneer, "They're convinced she wrote one, and in their mindless quest to follow a trend, they keep trying to order a book, which anyone with any real literary knowledge knows is nothing more than idle, ill-informed speculation."

"Why do you say that?" I asked, still trying to sound as innocent as possible.

He made a dismissive gesture with a hand,

"If there was such a thing, don't you think it would've been found by now? Somebody would've sold it and made an absolute fortune. No, it makes far more sense that, in the unlikely event it had ever existed - and that's a big if - it was most likely destroyed in the fire." He said in a worldly tone as he handed over my bag, "Regardless, I just wish the uninformed masses would do a little research before coming in here."

I was sure he was finished, but after furtively glancing around the shop, he unexpectedly leaned closer towards me.

"Although, between you and me, as long as people think they might find it, we are doing wonderful business here.

Profits are well up on last month, so it's almost worth listening to their foolhardy theories."

I half-smiled before quickly leaving both the shop and his misplaced certainty far behind. Once home again, I arranged them carefully in my bedroom alongside the picture of David. At first, I wanted nothing more than to read them all in rapid succession, but I resisted the temptation. I knew from experience the words contained within those pages were to be savoured, and I had plenty of time. But happy as I was to own more of her work, the journal was, without question, my most treasured possession and had a permanent home in my bedside table drawer, where I knew it would stay. For a fleeting moment, the thought did cross my mind that maybe I was being selfish, but I quickly reasoned that one day, long after I was gone, it might be found by someone, and then it would be for them to decide what was best.

Later that week, I attended an appointment with my therapist, which visibly surprised her when I appeared at her door. On the way there, I'd almost convinced myself that it would be best to tell her everything. But once I was sitting in her office, it felt as if I shared what had happened, it would be like betraying a sacred trust. So, instead, I credited reading books as having been the catalyst for the start of my recovery. Whether or not she entirely believed me, I couldn't be sure, but regardless, we arranged to see each other again. When I left, the earlier rain had stopped, and now the pale sun was struggling to shine through the remaining drifts of snow-coloured clouds. I strolled along the street and found myself wishing a couple of people 'a good day' as we passed each other. One nervously half-smiled back, whereas the other could barely hide their discomfort and pretended to be reading something intensely important on their phone. On reaching the park, I stopped and looked down towards the lake. Maybe because of the rain, there was hardly anyone there, giving the scampering squirrels and a myriad of small birds an undisturbed afternoon of foraging for food. Suddenly, on the far side, I saw two little girls, even though one was distinctly taller, they were dressed almost identically, both with large ribbon bows in their hair. They were chasing each other and laughing, but then, as I watched, suddenly, one stopped and looked in my direction. She raised her arm and waved to me, her action quickly copied by her companion.

My heart ached with a bittersweet joy, swollen with a poignant joy so sharp it brought stinging tears from my eyes. Before I had a chance to respond, they turned away and ran into the distance.

"I promise I won't fall, Miss Athena May Bower," I said quietly as they disappeared into the trees.

For a while, I was too caught in my own head to notice the rain had stopped, it was only when a single beam of sunlight pierced through the leaves that I came back to myself. A gentle breeze tousled my hair, laced with the fading scent of rain and sweet flowers. I blinked, noticing the flowers which shone like rainbow stars against a verdant green sky. As I passed, they bobbed their heads in greeting, leaves waving in a jubilant dance. Another ray of golden light curled past the trees that had me squinting, and I raised a hand to shield my eyes. How many times had I flinched from unfiltered brightness? Slowly, I lowered my hand and instead let my eyes adjust to the radiance. I watched how the light and shadow wove together, forming lace-like patterns on the pathway that shifted with each breath of air. I resumed walking, but this time, I kept my attention on the world around me- had the trees always been so green? Jewel-like from the rain, they glimmered as they swayed over my head. Dancers clothed in diamonds, the branches acting as their stage. A flash of movement called my attention away from the tall trees, I looked around, frowning slightly when I couldn't see anything different amongst the vivid flowers. As I watched, I saw one flutter slightly, and I felt my lips curl up in a grin. A butterfly. How many had I missed? Yet, as I paused to look, I wondered how I'd managed to ever ignore them. Delicate wings, the same orange hue as the flower it rested upon, opened as if to soak in the buttery-warm light. Everything about it seemed almost painfully fragile, from the delicate wings to the twin hair-like antennae. Impossibly so- as if nothing so breakable could live- yet here it was, against all odds. Beautiful.

As I meandered along, my thoughts began to unravel, like a spool of thread being gently pulled, memories and emotions intertwined in the recesses of my mind. Half-forgotten recollections rising to the surface of lazy afternoons in the sun beside the cheerful babbling fountain, how it had felt to laugh. I remembered the sharp sweetness of blackberries, ripened in the sun. How had I forgotten so much? The birds sang with renewed vigour as if they could see the dawn break within my own mind. Fresh light spilling over my thoughts. If I had such a thing, my soul seemed to exhale, and I wondered how long I'd been holding my breath.

As the sun began to slowly slip behind the trees, I reached the park entrance, knowing that, for now, my time in this magical place was over. I paused to glance back one more time before finally turning for home, still accompanied by the encouraging whispers of the loving breeze and melodic birdsong that sounded undeniably joyful despite the fading light. Perhaps they sang for the beauty of the sunset, or maybe to remind themselves it would rise once again. I still felt light despite leaving the park behind and the darkening sky.

For perhaps the first time in my life, with each step, I really heard them and understood them.

THE END

ABOUT THE AUTHOR

Born in West London, A.B. Turner had always written stories although it never occurred to her any of them would be published.

Her first novel was 'Hidden Within' and when this was released, it only served to make her start to believe that she could be an author. The novel became the first instalment of a trilogy and when the series was well-received, she truly began to spread her author wings. It was the book 'The Last Day' which marked the turning point in her writing career and gave her the confidence to push herself more with every subsequent work, fuelled by the belief she would hopefully improve with every story.

Aside from writing, she has travelled extensively, loves to cook and explore other forms of self-expression through art. So far, her life has been anything but dull and despite the numerous bumps in the road, she continues to seek new horizons.

She has many beliefs, but the main ones are 'never talk yourself out of doing anything' and 'only surround yourself with people who bring positivity with them.'

Printed in Great Britain
by Amazon

32345556R00146